Wanton Woman in White

URBAN LEGEND EROTICA COLLECTION

Wanton Woman in White

HONEY CUMMINGS

4 Horsemen
Publications, Inc.

Dedication

TABLE OF CONTENTS

1

THE BACHELOR

Remi Adama stared at his phone. His nerves tightened, mind spiraling in a mixture of emotions. On one hand, he could laugh at the ridiculous idea he had jumped into; on the other hand, he imagined it couldn't be any worse. After running from a bad relationship—*no, straight up abusive relationship that has evolved into a level five stalker situation—what do I have to lose?*

His phone buzzed, and he waited to see who was calling before answering. The screen lit up: *Show Bailey*. With a relieved sigh, he answered right away.

"Hey there, Bailey," he sounded cheerful, even excited. *Just get on with it.*

"Remi! Thank you for sending the contracts for the show back so fast," the Talent Coordinator said, her voice coolly professional. "In a moment, I will do a three-way call, and you and the mystery bride-to-be will have a moment to get acquainted. Mind you—there are rules involved."

"R-right," he stuttered, his nerves rising high once more. "So, in short, you guys are really marrying me to a stranger like some arranged marriage?"

"That's the gist of it," she chuckled. "We were having a hard time finding enough male contestants. A lot of them backed out after the phone calls, so... now we monitor them. Anyhow, who scouted you again? His information isn't on here."

"Oh, uh..." Remi scrambled through the scattered papers on his computer desk, knocking over a tower of empty pre-made boxes.

"A-are you okay?" Bailey had been startled by the sounds coming over the receiver.

"Y-yeah. It's just boxes for my online business." He found the piece of paper and squinted at his scribbled writing. Even with his glasses on, it seemed cryptic. "Man, my chicken scratch sucks ass... uh, Timmy? Tommy? No—Timmy. That's definitely an 'i' there."

"Huh. Timmy..." He could hear her rifling through paperwork and typing away on her keyboard. "Weird. We didn't have a Timmy listed... but I'll make a note." She finished a whirlwind of typing, paused, then continued. "Okay, now for the rules. You can't say names or locations of where you currently live. Talking about a hometown is okay... but no perverted or sexual commentary, or we'll terminate your contract. We do not payout on the contract until you tie the knot. If you need assistance to make the trip to the filming location in St. Augustine, Florida next week, please let me know."

"Right, right." Remi rubbed his forehead, eyebrows raised. "I need to be there some time on Friday, right? I'll be driving, so I just need the address. Text it to me if you can, Ms. Bailey."

"Absolutely, Remi." There was some tapping, and his phone buzzed. "Did it come through?" she asked.

"Perfect. Yes."

"Now, the three-way call."

Remi waited as he was placed on hold. His leg jittered, and

he glared at the boxes scattered across his tiny bedroom. With a grunt, he started to stack them, not noticing he had placed the smaller boxes on the bottom until he put the last box on top. Scoffing, he laughed at himself, leaning down to put his elbows on his knees.

"Remi?" Bailey's voice made him jolt, and he sat up, banging his head on his desk.

"Shit!"

"A-are you okay?"

"Y-yeah." Clearing his throat, he reassured her. "I was picking something off the floor. Sorry about that."

"Hi there," a softer, new voice cut across the receiver. "I guess we're getting married next week?"

"Uh, yeah. That seems to be the case." Remi leaned back in his chair, brow furrowing. "So... what do you do for a living?"

"Is he allowed to ask me that?" She sounded offended.

"He is." Bailey sighed, the sound blowing across the phone.

"Look, I run my own business out of my home," offered Remi, motioning to the towers of boxes filling the tiny apartment bedroom.

"Oh?" the sweet voice seemed intrigued. "And is it successful?"

Remi's muscles tensed as he pushed forward in the conversation. "Well, I guess that depends on your definition of success?"

"Money," she blurted in frustration. "Does it make a lot of money? It must not if you're still running it out of your room."

Remi blinked, shaking the shock off and defended himself. "It pays my bills. I'm not one of those guys who has a billion starter ideas and abandons them before getting them off the ground."

"Well, please understand, I want a man who can support me and the lifestyle I want to live."

Tilting his head, Remi tried again, "And what do you do for a living?"

"I'm unemployed. I intend to be a wife and nothing more or less." She sounded entitled. "As your beloved wife, I promise to always be at my best. Salon hair and nails dressed in the finest clothes and shoes. I am your trophy after all."

Eyes wide, Remi stuttered, "Wait, what?"

Shit. What kind of person am I about to be stuck with?

"We'll end the phone call here." Cutting in, Bailey dumped the bride-to-be off the phone. "You will get to meet her in person when you get to St. Augustine." She gave a nervous laugh.

"I see why the others bailed."

"Please! Look, I'll double the money." She dropped the bribe like a ton of bricks. "Remi, no one else is getting that offer from the show. You cannot disclose this deal with anyone. Marry her, and we'll pay you double."

Remi rubbed his forehead, "That's a lot of cash. I can buy a house and a car... and pay for an assistant." He looked around the room. "If she doesn't spend it first. I thought the money went to a joint venture?"

"We'll put half in a private account for only you," Bailey promised.

Silence fell. Remi covered his mouth, absorbing the offer. *They are desperate to marry this girl off, but why?*

"I've gotta ask," he inhaled deeply, "why not dissolve her contract if she's been so difficult rather than offer me double?"

Bailey groaned. "Okay, you can't say anything. Turns out she's the main investor's step-daughter, and he's shipping her out. She's been a mooch, and he's tired of her and figured the drama she would stir would make for great TV for the show."

"There it is." Remi smirked.

I can take advantage of this. The contract says we have to stay hitched for 180-days. I can milk it until then and annul the marriage. Yeah... yeah. I think I can do this. Why not? Treat myself since I can't seem to find a decent fucking woman.

"Triple it," he countered. "Double in the private account, so she stays out of it."

There was a long silence. "Let me put you on hold."

Remi shuffled the papers around on his desk. The coffee-stained copy of the contract revealed itself and he glanced through the pages for the price. At last he found it: *$300,000.00 USD.* Triple that, and he would almost have a million dollars. Granted, the crazy bride-to-be would be getting a third of that, but still...

Over half a million dollars. Now that should get me off the ground for good. Warehouse or no, just a bigger place should do it.

Bailey cleared her throat. "Mr. Adama?"

"Yeah?"

"We have a deal. Check your inbox for the revised contract, and this time, we're going to veri-sign digitally. There will be no getting out of this unless–" She choked, almost letting the name slip. "Unless the bride decides otherwise."

"Fine with me." Remi smiled ear to ear.

"The lawyer is revising it... so give it an hour or two to make it back your way." Bailey typed away on her keyboard. "Pleasure doing business with you, Mr. Adama. Look forward to seeing you in St. Augustine next week."

"Same–" Remi glared at the phone. "Huh, she hung up on me."

With a huff, he turned his attention back to his computer. Wiggling the mouse revealed a paused YouTube video, and he minimized that. Behind lay his prize: a porn site displayed tiles of all kinds of combinations and scenes. Clicking on one, he jumped the video ahead to where the girl dropped the last stitch of lingerie. Settling into his computer desk, it squeaked, and he took a pump of lotion. Slapping a hand towel like a ball net across his thighs, he leaned back, waiting for what would come next.

Another night, and another porn to keep me satisfied. No baggage, no bitching... the perfect jerk-bait girlfriend a man could ask for.

He watched, growing hard as the woman took a thick cock between her lips, gagging and drooling. Her enthusiasm to suck and choke on the baseball bat-sized dick only made him think of how easily she could take in his own cock. Closing his eyes, he focused on the moaning, slurping, and pop of lips. The heat and stiffness built as his thoughts dug deeper. He imagined her tongue wiggling under his shaft. Tightening his grip, he stroked faster, firmer. The gagging sounds shifting his imagination, and he could picture shoving himself deep into her mouth, holding her there as the tip...

With a groan, he released. Leaning forward, he folded the hand towel over and finished cleaning himself off. His phone buzzed and he reached for it, still in a haze. Riding out his euphoria, he didn't glance at the name on the screen before he answered.

"Remi!" Monica's voice sobered him quickly, and he sat up stiffly, wiping himself. "When are you going to give me my fucking cat back!"

"Are you kidding me?" Remi marveled. "You took him to the shelter a week before we broke up because he liked me more than you!"

Dammit, fell for it... shit.

"Oh! So you are going to talk to me, huh?" She seemed pleased to get a rise out of him.

"Look. I'm moving to Florida. We're done." He hung up.

Shit. Will this mystery bride be any better? Let's hope so...

2

THE WOMAN IN WHITE

The wind still held the heat of the day as it blew through Jenifer Rosalind's hair. Even late September in St. Augustine, Florida proved no different from a summer's day elsewhere in the world. Over the horizon, the sky faded from neon pink and orange to peach and lavender. She watched it from the same bridge over and over again.

She looked down to the creek, the current flowing fast beneath the bridge, but the water level was lower than it had been in previous seasons. Though the brackish water was on par with saltwater, the quality didn't keep the bullfrogs and catfish from swimming through the waterway, occasionally disturbing the calm surface. The cicadas screamed until at last they caved to the symphony of crickets and southern toads as the last sliver of sunlight faded.

The light pollution from the college area didn't completely wipe out the stars from where she stood alone. The breeze was already cooling down. Without the heat from the sun, the humid air quickly chilled at night, cutting right through her white wedding dress. Her skin, still damp from the day's heat, pebbled immediately, and she shuddered, cursing the lacy halter top and the thin fabric of the skirt's layers pressed hard against her legs. On the dark horizon, lightning chased itself through the incoming clouds. The moon and stars were swallowed, the spiderweb of white and orange streaks making bitterness rise in her gut.

Frowning, she looked down the bridge first one way, then the other, but she hadn't seen a car on it in months. Settling in the nook of railing, she smirked. Since it seemed she would be alone, and bored out of her mind, what better way could she pass the time other than...? She bit her lip, inching the skirts up and over her knees.

"Dammit, I'm so pale I fucking glow," she muttered, awestruck as ever at the sight of her skin.

Shaking her head, she regained her aim. Fingers slid between her thighs, and she leaned back into the icy metal that braced her. Raising a foot, she balanced her leg to gain greater access to the pink jewel she desired. Her skirts flapped in the wind, and in the distance, a whippoorwill sang loudly between the rumbles of thunder. With the incoming thunderstorm, the temperature fell even more rapidly, a good ten or more degrees as the humidity left her skin sticky.

Goosebumps rolled across her skin, nipples hard as her fingers glided over her opening. She was slick with her wanton desire, the loneliness and thoughts of being taken. A bride abandoned on this very bridge during a hurricane ages ago, all she wanted was to rid herself of the past, to move on, and to be taken by a man worthy of her body.

So tired of doing this...

She inhaled, fingers dipping between her folds, thrusting and rubbing. Her leg jittered, and she slid her fingertips out, hot and wet as they began circling her clit. The swollen, hard jewel rose to the occasion. Electricity shot through her in tandem with a lightning strike. Thunder vibrated through the steel so cold and wet through the skirts of her dress. She arched, her orgasm rising. Head drooped back, eyes shut tight, she inhaled sharply.

A little more...

Icy raindrops started to pitter and patter all around. One hit her cheek, prompting her to speed up. Biting her lip, she moaned, trying desperately to draw the orgasm forward. The rain thickened, spattering her exposed legs, arms, and...

Fuck me!

Abandoning her play, she rose to her feet and threw a bird to the sky, "Fuck you too!"

Rain thick and hard fell relentlessly across Jenifer and her world. The creek was no longer visible from the bridge. Nothing but the pouring rain, wind, and thunder filled the air where once nature had played a sweet serenade to her. Crossing her arms, teeth chattering, she stood in the middle of the bridge with nowhere to go and nowhere for shelter... *again.*

Stumbling to the middle of the bridge, she faced south and frowned.

If I could go that direction, it would take me home. Would I even have a place to go back to?

Twisting, she faced north where the road curved up a small hillside.

If I could go that way, it would take me to the old farmhouse. Granted, I was supposed to be married there, but they might take me in. Surely that place is still open to travelers?

Looking down at her feet, she huffed. They were pale and ghostly... a*nd growing brighter?*

She turned and saw headlights coming at her fast. The wheels squealed and skidded across the wet road. Wide eyed, she watched as the man at the wheel struggled to turn. He swerved around her, and she covered her mouth, chasing the brake lights as he hydroplaned to the other end. By some small miracle, he managed not to ping-pong off the railing and at last exited the bridge and high-centered on the curb.

The little blue *(Or was it purple?)* Ford Focus teetered as the man stumbled out. He held his head, walking backwards to assess his car in the rain and wind. At last, he spun and shouted something. Jenifer blinked, impressed she could hear him this far with a thunderstorm in full swing. He ran full stride back down the length of the bridge. Gripping her shoulder, he looked her over, his face smooshed as he squinted.

"Are you okay? I didn't hit you, did I?"

"So loud!" Jen lowered her brow, wondering if something had happened to affect her hearing.

"Sorry, I just... dammit, I can't see shit without my glasses." He glanced over her again and looked all around. "You're not hurt? I don't need to get help, do I?"

"I'm fine, but..." Jen pushed him back, the rain and pitch dark night making it hard to pick apart his features. "Who are you? What are you doing driving down this bridge so late?"

"I'm Remi. Look, Miss...?" He was shouting over the weather.

"Jenifer," she offered.

"Miss Jenifer, I was going to ask you why you were standing here in the rain so late," he retorted. "Here, let's get in the car and out of the rain, so we don't have to shout over the–"

Thunder muted his words, and before she could say anything else, he tugged her along by her hand. As they reached the threshold where the bridge met the paved road, she slipped from his grip. She stared, nervous and unknowing at the line the two made. In the past, she had tried to take a step, to dare to push herself to make the rest of the trip to the old farmhouse, but inevitably, it failed or she'd feel faint.

It's not that I didn't want to get married; it's just the weather got so bad...Then the storm surge sent the creek–

"Come on. It's okay. I don't care if that piece of shit gets wet."

10

Remi scooped her around the waist and thrust her forward.

"W-wait..." she sputtered, looking over her shoulder in confusion. "How did you...?"

"Here." He shoved her into the passenger side and shut the door.

Jenifer watched him with growing interest as Remi slid in the car with water dripping from his goatee. She couldn't help herself. "Who are you again? Are you even from here? *Why* are you out here?"

"Me?" Remi pointed at himself, his brow furrowed. "I'm Remi. And you're... Yennefer?"

"Jenifer. We already exchanged names, Remi." She narrowed her eyes at him, noticing how his gaze didn't seem to focus on her. "Where are you going?" Twisting, she glanced back behind her, trying to look out the window. "What are you even looking at?"

"Uh, good question." He scrambled around the tiny car, bumping into her leg. "S-sorry, just... oh, here it is. My phone's GPS stopped working, and all I remember is Bailey saying to go over a bridge and the farmhouse was just up the way."

"Y-you're going to the farmhouse?" She leaned in closer, enjoying the heat of his body so close to hers. *When was the last time I even felt another person's body heat? Before my accident? Wait, this is my chance to make it to the farmhouse! Just maybe this curse can be broken after all!* "Please take me with you! I'm headed there, too!"

"Is that why you were standing out there?" Shuffling around, he reached below the dashboard and came back up with glasses. "Found them."

"Well, you could say I was stuck on the bridge for having cold feet." Jen laughed nervously.

Remi cleaned the lenses and pulled on his glasses. The lightning flashed, and as they locked eyes, Remi inhaled sharply.

Jenifer cringed, the reaction making her fear the worst. His eyes flowed over her, down and up again before at last, he smiled. *Last time a man shot me that look...* She tilted her head, visible confusion building on her face.

"You're a bride?" Remi scoffed. "I can't believe they'd leave you wandering around out here like this. And in a storm!"

"Yes, but I was the one who..." He flipped on the dome light, and she blinked. *My Adonis... I have found you!*

He was handsome. Nothing like her former fiancée, this man looked strong, like he could build a barn solo if he had no other choice in the matter. Her eyes slid over his thick hands, muscular arms, and at last lingered on his plump lips. Reaching out, her fingertips caressed the heat of his arm, and he visibly shuddered. As she crested his shoulder, his other hand cupped hers.

"So warm..." she whispered.

"Wow, you're cold." He twisted to the back of the car, cursing under his breath. "I don't have anything in the back... I might have a jacket in the trunk. I can go get it... hold on."

Lightning lit the car up once more, and her pale face reflected in his glasses for a split-second, gaunt and ghostly. He reached for the car door, stuttering about the jacket in disjointed bits. Jenifer gripped his shirt and pulled him back to her, across the tiny center console. He spun and their lips locked. She deepened the kiss, his lips parting. Willingly, he teased the tip of her tongue before overpowering her. With a jerk, it ended, his hands on her shoulders with a wild expression.

"We're supposed to wait until we get married first!" he exclaimed.

"Wait, what?"

What in the blazes is he going on about?

3

LATE ARRIVAL

Remi's heart beat loud and fast. He couldn't tell if his movements or the storm winds outside made the tiny Focus rock on the curb, teeter-tottering here and there. Regardless, he clutched the strange bride before him. His glasses were starting to fog up. He flung them onto the dashboard and kissed her once more.

Who am I to resist? She's so damn gorgeous and...

She crawled across the car, the Focus shifting with a clunk as it tilted hard. An icy hand gripped his wrist and shoved his palm onto her breast. Remi squeezed, and she deepened the kiss, moaning. Her other hand slid down his torso and rubbed the hardening length under his zipper. He broke the kiss off once more.

"Wait-wait-wait-wait," he muttered, the cramp and confined quarters making it clear it would be near impossible to have sex. "There's not enough room to... you know..." He motioned at her dress and the backseat filled with boxes. "I didn't buy the Focus for fucking..." He cringed.

"Oh." Jenifer took in the cramped situation, her dress filling up her side of the car. "Oh! Oh no." She turned her attention back to Remi. "But you're hard already, and," she winced, "it's all my fault."

"Look, when we get to the farmhouse—" Remi looked away, cursing his glasses on the dashboard, her face blurred and unreadable. "We can hook up, but it's gotta be secret."

"R-right, but still, I think there's enough room for at least this." Her fingers were quick, his pants unfastened and her hands gripping his hard-on in a few seconds.

"Dammit!" he cursed, surprised and shocked, but glad he never bothered with underwear.

"What's wrong?" She looked up at him, all doe-eyed, and his heart fluttered.

Shaking in admiration, he mumbled, "Y-your hands are cold."

"But not my mouth," she winked, leaning down.

Remi moaned as his cock slid into the wet heat of her mouth. Her tongue wiggled and rubbed on the underbelly of his shaft, sending chills across his entire being. At last, the tip of his cock hit the back of her throat, and she sucked hard, letting him linger there. Pulling off his dick, she stopped at the cap, tongue circling once, twice, and repeating the slow motion over and over. He moaned each time he connected to the back of her throat, his balls tensing with the urge to come.

Fingers gently caressed his testicles, and he groaned, becoming rock-hard. He cursed, unable to shift into a more comfortable position. He already had the seat all the way back for driving and... She picked up speed, and he fought the urge to hold her down on his cock. He gripped the steering well, head tilting back, his eyes closing.

His cell phone started ringing.

Alarmed, Jenifer pulled off his dick with a pop. "What is that?"

"M-my phone." He caved and glanced at the screen: *Show*

Bailey. "Shit, it's the Coordinator." Reluctantly, he picked it up. "B-bailey."

"Mr. Adama, where are you? It's an hour past midnight, and you were supposed to be here by now." She sounded beyond pissed. "We had an agreement, or do you intend to back out of our deal?"

"Whoa-whoa-whoa-whoa." Now Remi sounded miffed. "I am stuck over by the bridge."

"The bridge?" she echoed.

"Yea, I almost hit a woman on the bridge, but we're both okay. My car's stuck on the cur—" Remi's words faltered as Jenifer began stroking his cock.

She gave sheepish grin as he looked down at her. *Is this a challenge? To see if I can sustain my conversation while she plays with my dick?*

"Stuck where, Mr. Adama?" Bailey's voice made him inhale, trying to fight the building pleasure.

"The curb right after you cross." His voice broke some as a hot tongue licked the length of his shaft from the base to the tip.

"I see. I suppose the storm is rather bad tonight." Bailey babbled about a possible *tropical storm,* but Remi couldn't focus on her words.

Jenifer began kissing and licking his dick in earnest. He relished the way her lips felt hot and soft against his hardened strength, the lashing of her tongue and warm breath washing over him. A moan escaped him, and he dropped the phone. Jenifer snickered, handing it back to him.

"R-Remi? Remi?" Bailey's voice blasted loud over the receiver.

Fumbling with the phone, Remi finally replied, "Y-yes! I-I dropped the phone."

"Are you in pain?" Bailey seemed concerned.

"Wait, what?" Remi furrowed his brow and stifled a moan as Jenifer went down on him.

"Y-you're groaning an awful a lot." She declared.

"Am I?" He gripped the steering wheel, biting his lip as his cock connected with the back of her throat. "Well..." She began thrusting up and down his shaft, and he teetered with the car on the edge of an orgasm. "I can't...." He inhaled swiftly, fighting the urge to come. "I can't..." He was sweating from his battle of sheer will to hold back. "I..."

"Can't what?" demanded Bailey.

"The car. It's stuck! Send help!"

Lightning flashed as he hung up and threw the phone on the dash next to his glasses. "Fuck, I'm..."

Jenifer pulled all of him into her mouth, sucking hard, tongue rubbing purposefully against his shaft as she deep-throated his cock. White-knuckled grip on the steering wheel, Remi moaned, cumming into her sealed suction of his cock. She pushed down, swallowing, and he groaned again. At last she slid slowly and purposefully off. He panted and relief washed over him, his grip releasing the steering wheel.

"Feel better?" she chuckled.

"That was harder to do than I expected." He laughed. "I was trying to let you know..."

"I know. And no offense, I could tell." She leaned back in her chair and stared out the window as the storm continued. "So, who was that? Your bride?"

"No, no, that was Bailey the Talent Coordinator. Surely you've talked to her too?" Remi tucked himself away, zipping his pants as a flash of headlights appeared. "Shit, we weren't far from the farmhouse after all."

"N-no. It's just behind the sand dune there." Jenifer frowned. "I suppose this is where we part ways."

"Wait, you're giving up just like that?" A SUV came to a stop behind the teetering Focus that clunked when he shifted to look. "Look, I bet that's the production crew coming to get us both."

He couldn't see her face, scrambling for his glasses on the dash. "I get the feeling you're giving me sad eyes. My sight is shit."

"Remi, you should know, I'm really a—" The car horn honked, muting her words.

"I know, I know. A bride for the show. Look, I'm a groom. Granted, we're not each other's bride and groom..." Another honk. "Let me run out there and see if they have space for us both."

Before Jenifer could say much more, Remi rushed out into the thunderous storm. The rain fell in large icy drops, lightning lighting the area up. He got out of the car, which teetered on the chassis and seemingly had no wheels on the ground. Cursing under his breath, he ran to the SUV and cracked the door open. The 90s emo male intern blinked at him, jerking in the driver seat.

"You have room for two of us?" he demanded.

"Y-yeah?" His reply was almost too low to be heard over the pelting rain, squeaking windshield wipers, and rolling thunder.

Remi wasted no time, spinning back to the Focus. He hurried to the passenger side and threw the door open, startling Jenifer. He grabbed her hand and pulled her along through the darkness. She tightened her grip on his grip, looking up at him in wonder. He pushed her into the passenger side of the SUV and spun, turning back.

Shit, my keys! I left the car running like a moron. Remi made his way back to the car, turning off the ignition, and taking the keys with him.

By the time he pulled himself into the SUV, water dripped from his beard, and his clothes and body clung to the vinyl seats. He squeaked into place. Pulling on the seat belt, Jenifer and the intern spun to glare at him in the back. His face flushed.

"Okay, let's go," he said, hoping it would prompt them to stop staring.

"The headlights," announced Jenifer.

"You left the headlights on. The battery will die, won't it?" added the intern.

Remi turned, squinting to see the rocking Focus with its lights on. "Fuck me!"

With a huff, he slung the seatbelt back off and went back out to weather the storm once more. He scrambled to the driver's side, flipping the headlights off and grabbing his ringing cell phone off the dash. Lightning flashed and he winced, the strike so close the thunder shook the ground at his feet and the air in his lungs. Shaking it off, he climbed back into the SUV, panting. He felt drained.

The intern's cell phone rang, and he picked up, "Yeah, I got him and the missing bride. We're heading back now, Ms. Bailey." Hanging back, he looked back at Remi. "Anything else you need?"

"Nah, man." Remi shook his head. "It can all wait until tomorrow when it's not raining."

The SUV started to make its U-turn. "Hate to say it, but there's a tropical storm slowly making its way in. This is just the precursor. Granted, tomorrow you might be able to get things between rain bands. Oh, and I think Ms. Bailey made arrangements for a tow truck to bring the car to the farmhouse."

"Wait, we're going to the farmhouse?" Jenifer panicked.

"Y-yeah?" Remi and the intern replied in confusion.

Jenifer covered her mouth then at last pulled her hands away. "Sorry. I guess you could say wedding jitters, still?" She gave a nervous laugh. "I made it this far so... why not the farmhouse?"

"You're weird." The intern rolled his eyes and pulled in front of the old two-story house that could pass for a vintage hotel.

"I like weird girls. I mean..." Remi covered his face, realizing that he'd left his glasses in the car. *That came out all wrong.*

"And I like men who are willing to wade through a storm without question," she countered, laughing.

4

FARMHOUSE FOLLY

Walking into the entrance of the Farmhouse, Jenifer froze. The space was nothing like she remembered. Candleholders were long gone, and the new electricity ran everywhere. Large wires were taped to the wooden floors, black lines running to the clusters of film equipment setup everywhere she looked. The walls had been painted, furniture changed, and entire area far more embellished than when she had visited with her fiancée. Looking down at her bare feet, she marveled at her surroundings.

I made it. From the bridge, I finally made it this far after over a hundred years.

"Remi!" A middle-aged red-head exploded from a corridor, the woman locking eyes with Jenifer as she stumbled to a stop. "You're not Remi..." She looked Jenifer up and down. "And you're not Karen either."

"I can leave..." Jenifer offered slowly, her chest aching at the idea.

"Wait. She may be a no-show after all." The glimmer in the woman's eyes made Jenifer's eye twitch. *I know a conman, or woman, when I see one.*

"Bailey! Thank for sending someone so fast!" Remi's voice boomed through the old farmhouse, echoing against the walls. Jenifer thought the display of wine glasses clattered.

"Hush! Everyone is asleep," hissed Bailey, holding up a finger. She turned to her cell phone, thumb swiping left and right. "Mystery bride, what's your name? Who was your recruiter?"

"Jenifer and... recruiter?" she tried, stepping backward, but managed to bump into Remi. His heavy hands fell on her shoulders. *Dammit, I'm trapped.*

"Are you not signed up?" Remi paled when she gritted her teeth and mouthed *no.* "It was Timmy, right?" he said confidently.

"T-timmy?" Jenifer and Bailey asked in unison.

"Your recruiter, like me. It was Timmy. I thought that's what you said in the car?" Remi spun Jenifer to face him and lipped, *say yes.*

"Y-yes, Timmy." Jenifer's voice shook.

"Ah, not that guy. I can't find his information... that means you don't have a contract written up either!" Holding her head, Bailey paced back and forth. "The producer is going to kill me! First, the investor's daughter is a no-show, no-call, no-answer... and now I have a non-contracted bride drenched in rain almost run over by one of our grooms! This has workman's comp written all over it!"

Jenifer shuddered once, then twice. She hadn't done that since...

Am I cold? I haven't been cold since the day I...

She leaned into Remi, the heat of his body against hers making her blood rush. *What on earth is happening to me?* She pinched her arm. *Dammit, that hurt. Holy crap...*

"I'm... I am..." Jenifer's teeth were chattering, her words struggling.

"Hey, she's freezing." Remi wrapped his arms around her. "Anywhere she can change close by, maybe a hot shower?"

Covering her mouth, Bailey's eyes searched the air for several minutes as she considered. They waited, and she finally shrugged, shaking her head. "Whatever. Sure. Straight back this way. She can take Karen's room. Bobby, show them where it is." With a glance at Jenifer's wedding dress, she added, "There should be some spare sweats for everyone on the table when you pass."

Bobby, their emo-driver from before, pushed past them, and they followed in silence. The old wooden floors creaked underfoot as they climbed the stairs to the divided hallway. There, as promised, was a table filled with all kinds of amenities. Toothpaste, shampoo, and sweats bearing the show's logo were piled in a glorious mini-buffet of necessities.

Remi stopped, strangely excited about all of it, but Jenifer kept walking with Bobby. He opened a door at the end of the hall and smirked, studying her from head to toe, taking in the shape of her body beneath the semi-transparent gown. Running a hand through his hair, he glanced at Remi, the larger man loading his arms up with goodies and clothes from the table.

"How about you and I ditch this geek and have a little fun before you tie the knot?" He flicked his eyebrows for good measure as he surveyed her again, more slowly this time.

"Uh, no thanks." Jenifer's annoyance made the lights flicker, and she held her breath.

"Look, I got you a tiny shampoo." Remi had caught up to them. He glanced up at the flickering light above their heads. "Man, old houses seem to have the worst electrical problems."

The lights stopped buzzing as his hand hit her shoulder. "Is this the room where we can take a shower?"

"Y-yeah." Bobby the intern paled, looking small in comparison to how Remi towered behind her, adding to her ominous presence. "Otherwise you'd have to use the community bath-room on the other end of the hall. This is the master bedroom–"

"Alright!" Remi pushed past him, pushing Jenifer through the door in front of him. He closed the door in the emo-kid's face and rushed to unload his prize pickings onto the bed. The room was arranged around the large bed, a dresser pressed against the far wall and a desk tucked into a corner beneath the wide window. A small lamp sat on the desk, the dim light bathing the room. There was a wooden door in the wall to her right, probably leading to a private bathroom.

Jenifer smirked, admiring the excitement he carried for the smallest of treats.

He's a groom. I'm a bride. And for one night I'm alive to do—what exactly? Screw this. I know what I've been dying to do...

Biting her lip, she reached behind her and locked the door. By the time she tip-toed into reach, he had separated his items from what he had grabbed for her, and the gesture made her pause. Tilting her head, she looked at the display as he spun around, eyes sparkling and grin wide on his face.

"There! I suppose you should use the shower first," he announced, puffing out his chest in pride. He frowned as he saw the look on her face. "W-wait, what are–"

A devilish smirk crossed her lips as she untied the ribbon that cinched the waist, slipping the wet wedding dress off first one shoulder and then the other. The fabric slid down her body, the train sewn to the waist piling in waves of white, and she stepped out of it, moving closer to him. "Before that, there's something I want to do..."

"Look, we just met and..." Remi stumbled as the dress fell heavily on the ground. His eyes followed it, then scanned hun-grily upwards. At last, he breathed, "Dammit, you're gorgeous."

Jenifer reached out to run her hands down his torso, her ghostly fingers bypassing his clothes to glide over his skin. A shudder shook his shoulders, and she pushed her body closer to his, relishing the heat of a living body. A twinkle of her nose, and his pants unfastened and fell to the floor. He jolted in surprise, taking a step back and out of his pants to land awkwardly against the bed. She pushed him into a sitting position. Shaking his head but still smiling, he pulled his shirt off, muttering about his missing glasses.

He flung his wet shirt to the ground with a thud, and Jenifer straddled his lap. Their lips locked, her hand snaking between them until she gripped his hardened shaft. Remi moaned, his tongue deepening their kiss as she began stroking him. His big arms pulled her against him, the heat of his body making her feel alive again. Her wanton desire made her impatient.

I've waited a good century for a wedding night like this and in this very farmhouse no less!

Arching back, she broke their kiss. Eyes locked, she guided his cock inside her pussy. The pleasure on his face thrilled her as she let him slide slowly and purposefully deeper. Hot fingers trailed down the line of her spine before resting on her hips. He pulled her forward, a firm and knowing direction and pushed deeper inside her. A gasp escaped her, the sensation invigorating and satisfying.

She rocked, his hands showing her when to grind forward and arch backward. The lightning from the storm outside lit the room, shadows of their bodies moving together illuminated in quick flashes. Rolling thunder let her moan her pleasure. Her fingers lingered near where he entered her, and she enjoyed feeling him there inside her. Remi licked and suckled at her breast, his own pleasure muffled by her flesh. Her body buzzed with the rising orgasm, her blood running hot as her heart thudded loud.

I feel so... so... alive.

Fingers slick from her pussy, she began circling her swollen clit. "You feel so amazing..." she told him.

She tightened, and Remi released her nipple to moan, "You're so... so..."

He seemed breathless, and she pushed him back into his treasure trove of toiletries. "I want you to watch me ride your cock."

"O-okay." His hands slid across her hips and gripped her thighs.

She wiggled into position, allowing his dick to slide in and out of her as she bounced on top of him. Her breasts moved with the motion, leaning back so her fingers could continue their play. His fingers dug into her thighs, his cock growing stiffer inside her. She slowed, sitting firmly on him until every inch of his dick was inside her. Arching back, she rolled her fingers over her clit harder, firmer. Her pussy tightened hard on his shaft, and it jumped with excitement. Grinding against him, she could feel her orgasm building with each circle.

"So tight..." moaned Remi.

"Oh I wanted this so bad..." she breathed. "A big cock inside me..."

Remi smirked. "You like how that feels, hm?"

"Don't you move!" she demanded, her other hand gripping her breast. "I'm... I'm almost there."

The heat of his hand slid up to her other breast, pinching it. "Let me help."

"Oh, touch me more," she pleaded.

"If you insist," he rocked under her, making his cock rub inside her pussy. "When I'm done, you'll be begging me to stop."

"Please... I want..." Her breath caught, her pussy tight with her orgasm as she lunged forward.

FINALLY! A REAL ORGASM!

5

THE BATHROOM

Wrapping his arms around her, Remi pulled her body into him and thrust hard and fast. She felt so amazing, so tight and wet. *The way she looks so haunting on top of me like that...*

Seeing her touch herself had been more than enough to make him agonize over coming too soon. Biting his tongue, he fought to hold it back, wanting to make her come one more time. She shrieked like a banshee, arching in his arms, nipples hard and pressing into his chest.

Her skin was on fire, finally warming up. A gush and another tight lock on his cock signaled she had come once more in the short window of wanton peak. He pushed her back, lifting her off him onto his thighs, and gripped his cock with a grunt. He looked left and right. Everything was a blur, but he didn't want to dump his load in the only dry clothes they had.

"Shit, I need something to release in!" He groped at things, hating that he couldn't see shit without his glasses.

Hot lips wrapped around the top of his dick and sucked. She shoved his hands away, taking his cock all the way in as he released. This time his breath caught as she made his own orgasm linger longer. Again, she swallowed, and he moaned at the way her tongue danced against the length of his shaft. He rocked in and out of her lips, slowly as the last ejaculation let go. Jenifer pulled her mouth off his cock, and they looked at one another, both grinning broadly.

"Feel better?" she offered.

"Oh yeah," he inhaled, holding a deep breath for a moment before huffing it out. "You seem to have had a good time of it."

"I'm not done," she warned, beginning to kiss her way back up his body.

"Uh, you do know it takes a man a while to recharge, right?" He marveled at how enthralling her lips felt against his torso.

I've done this to a woman plenty of times, but on me... holy hell I've been missing something in my life!

"What if I told you I might know a way to..." She paused and looked at him, eyes glowing in the haze of his blurry vision.

Is that the lighting in here? Or are my eyes really getting this bad?

"...speed things along," she offered, her fingers beginning to stroke his dick once more.

"Look, I've heard great things about Viagra, but I'm not that kind of guy," he confessed.

Jenifer stopped and sat up. "What is Viagra?"

"Uh, the little blue pill that makes you rock-hard for like hours on end?" He couldn't believe she had no idea. "Like on the late night infomercials?"

"Forgive me. I've literally been stuck in the middle of nowhere while the world grew around me." She crossed her arms, and the dim desk light began to flicker.

"Oh." Remi bit his lip. *Dammit, I ruined the moment. Now what?* "I'm sorry?" he offered.

Her body language softened, arms uncrossing. "It couldn't

be helped. And why are you apologizing?"

"I just assumed everyone knew what Viagra was." He shrugged, shifting his body and making some of the toiletries fall off the bed. "Huh. You'd think they would have fallen sooner?"

"Let's fuck some more." Her voice darkened, and he caught her gaze as icy fingers gripped his cock.

Grunting, he pulled her hand away. "First, you need to warm up in the shower. I mean, you're as cold as a dead body, girl."

He pulled himself to his feet and tugged her behind him. "But Remi..."

"But nothing." His authoritative tone silenced her.

Guiding her along, he managed to push her through the bathroom threshold and flip on the light switch, revealing white tiles and golden fixtures. She gasped, spinning slowly to take in the entire room. He chuckled to see her eyes light up. The huge shower space, the deep garden tub, and monster-sized vanity had her eyes wide with wonder. She rushed to each one, afraid to fully touch it but desperate to reaffirm they were indeed real.

"If you want, I can take the shower and you can take the tub?" Remi suggested. Jenifer spun around and scowled at him. "Or I take the tub?" he tried.

"No, *WE* are taking a bath *together*," she announced.

She looks way too excited about this idea. I can't tell her no. I mean... she swallowed twice for me now!

Jenifer moved as if to leave the room, and he caught her arm. "Whoa, where are you going?"

"To fetch water." She blinked. "To fill the tub?"

"This may be an old house, darling," he winked, strutting over the fixtures, "but it is up to speed on the basic utilities."

Her eyes widened as he turned the knobs and water came spewing out. "They have indoor plumbing!"

"Y-yeah..." He tilted his head in confusion as she rushed over to dip her hands in.

"And it's hot water!" She gasped, laughing as she stepped into the tub. "This must have cost them a fortune!"

"I guess, since the house wasn't built with it?" Remi shrugged her reaction off. *She must have been brought up by...* "Are you Amish by chance?"

"Amish?" She made a face. "Do you think an Amish girl would suck cock like that?"

He laughed, choking on his own spit.

"Oh, you okay?"

He waved her off, sliding into the tub across from her.

As the huge space began to fill with hot water, he scanned the assortment of bath oils and bubbles lined up on a small shelf along the wall. A grin crossed his face. *Lavender bubbles for the win.* He dumped half the bottle under the flowing water without thinking. The reaction was immediate, a white plume of bubbles that had them both in a fit of giggles until soon Remi couldn't see her... or the bathroom any more. He had poured too much, the volatile concoction far more potent than the dime-store brands he had encountered in the past. The bubbles towered up like some elephant toothpaste chemistry experiment and toppled onto the tiled floor. He swam in them, hands reaching for Jenifer and nearly smacked her in the face.

"Shit! I poured too much!" He paled, but she only laughed harder, kissing him firmly on the lips for a quick second.

"I think this is wonderful!" Her hands cupped his face, her smile making his heart flutter.

"Y-you do?" he blinked. *If I could just read her expression a little more clearly...did I leave my glasses in the car or on the bridge?*

Another kiss planted on his lips, and Jenifer's tongue dipped into his mouth. They licked at one another, the water sloshing as he blindly groped for the knob to shut off the faucet. Her thighs hugged his hips, and he slipped backward until the garden tub caught his back. Slick with bubbles, his hand explored the curves of her body, squeezing and groping, chasing how her body dipped and bloomed. She broke the kiss, giggling again as she wiped bubbles from her face.

Catching a nipple in his lips, he pulled her to him, water slapping against the tub from the motion. She yelped, and he sucked more hungrily. Her fingers pulled him into her breast, goading him on. His teeth teased the hardened nipple, and she gasped. He was getting hard again, and Jenifer reacted. Her hips slid her pussy against the hardened shaft, making waves in the massive tub for two. Both moaned as she shifted, and he slipped inside her. The water added to the heat of the moment, while the bubbles made them blind to one another. Hands gliding across slick planes of flesh without direction, groping and pulling one another closer.

He released her nipple and moved over to the other breast. She tightened on his cock, and he shuddered in delight. Widening his mouth, he took in more of her breast. He rocked his hips, matching her rhythm so he could push deeper inside her. Water slapped across the tub's edge, spilling as it splashed against the tile.

"Faster," she breathed. "I want you to fuck me faster. I'm almost... I'm almost there."

Releasing her breast, he couldn't see her through the bubbles. "I can't at this angle."

"Then change angles!" She gently cleared bubbles, searching for the tub edge. "What if I lean over?"

Remi shuffled onto his knees, the water slapping the tub walls from his rush. "That might just work..."

His hands gripped her hips, lining her up. Straightening himself, he came too short with the way she had bent over the edge. Blowing bubbles from his mouth, he wiped more away, but still managed to smack her ass. She yelped, and when no rebuttal came, he smirked and repeated the action a few more times. Rubbing her ass cheeks with a red blush forming, he dipped his fingers between her thighs.

When his finger rolled over her clit, her thighs tensed. He pressed on, rolling and rubbing the opening of her wet pussy. The water and bubbles added to the surreal moment. *I shouldn't be doing this... but dammit, I might be stuck with a real Karen for the rest of my life instead of...*

He dipped his fingers into her pussy, thrusting hard and fast. Jenifer was on her tippy-toes, squealing with delight. His arm ached, and at last, he broke away and returned his grip to her hip.

"Bend your knees," he told her. He wanted back inside her, his cock throbbing with want. "I can't reach. You're too high."

"Oops." She began bending her knees when—*pop!* "FUCK ME!"

"I'm trying!" Remi's heart raced. *Shit, she's pissed!*

6

She's Back

Pain rolled through her, destroying the arousal. Her knee locked up, no different than it had done in her living state. It all came back in a blinding flash, thunder rolling outside to match the peak of her frustration. She turned, palmed Remi's chest, but his eagerness to rise to his feet and grip her made it clear that he misunderstood her words in the throes of passion.

"My knee... I can't..." she choked back the tears. At last, she saw recognition cross his face. "I forgot how much this hurts..."

Without a word, he scooped her up. She curled into him, hissing with each bounce of his step. He slid in the bubbles, but at least she still had the ability to move objects and righted him with a twinkle of her nose. All she wanted was to let him cradle her in this moment of pain.

She had fallen off the horse, slamming her knee on the only godforsaken rock in the whole damn field. After that point, it never healed right, and worse, she couldn't always bend it. Her toes numbed as another shot of pain made her press harder against his chest.

31

"I got you. It's going to be okay," he cooed, his voice soft and affectionate, making her heart swell.

I've never had a man talk to me like this before...

He set her on the bed gently, walked back to the bathroom and returned, handing her a fuzzy towel. "Here. I'll go grab some ice..." He rushed to put on the sweats with the obnoxious pink logo reading *Love at First Married.* He spied the open bathroom door. "Crap. Let me close this... the bubbles are dying down but..." He shut the door and the room fell dark with only the dim desk light. "Let me go get ice... I'll be right back. I promise."

With that, he left her alone in the room. She blinked, staring at her swelling knee awestruck. Trying to shift on top of the assortment of toiletries, she winced. The pain brought her back to the day she had fallen off the bridge, swept away with the storm surge. Lightning flashed outside, the wind slapping rain across the window as if agreeing with her.

This is usually the moment I fade away and wake up back on the bridge—or relive the moment.

A chill sent her body into a shudder, and she wrapped the towel tighter around her body. That night, it had stormed like this, but first thing in the morning, she was to marry Beau D. Phallis, the farmer's eldest son. As if by some twist of fate, a storm had blown in fast and hard. It always stormed hard during August, so no one thought anything of it. Her mother hemmed her dress up a little higher so the puddles wouldn't ruin the lace edging. She even pinned the train up for good measure, tucking it behind her.

"Momma, we can reschedule." Jenifer frowned in the mirror at herself before catching the disgruntled glare on her mother's face. "There's no telling when this storm will end."

"True, Babydoll, but I'm not cancelling this wedding. We've already made the food. People are already pouring into Phallis

Farm, and they came to see two people get married—today." She finished connecting the train up so it wouldn't drag on the ground. "We'll cut this thread lose once you get into the house over there."

"But Momma," her voice lowered, "what if it's a sign?"

"A sign?" her mother scoffed. "To have the wedding inside? Absolutely! Remember how Rebecca fainted two summers ago at her uncle's funeral? August is a terrible time to wear a dress this elaborate."

"Did you just compare my wedding dress to funeral attire?" She spun with disbelief. "This is all a sign. It has to be."

"For what, Jenny?" Her mother snorted, hands on hips now.

"That... that..." Jenifer's chest tightened, and she couldn't hold her tongue. "We're not meant to marry one another."

"Whoa, did I ever walk in at the wrong time," Michael, her older brother, choked on the cupcake he had snuck from the kitchen.

"Michael van Winkle!" Before either of them could react, her mother had closed the gap and started shooing her brother out of the room. "You are not to ruin this day for your sister! Go get the wagon!"

"Well, Momma, I came to bring you over first. There's no room left thanks to Aunt Cathy being as big as Jimmy's prized sow." Jenifer and he chuckled hysterically, earning heated glares powerful enough to silence them.

"Boy, you better apologize to my sister in the buggy." Her mother paused, turning to Jenifer and looking to the window where lightning flashed. "There should be room for Jenny."

"Big Jo is too spooked over the thunder. We don't need a runaway horse and buggy with a bride in it. So only little Penny seems willing to pull it. Just one horse and..."

"Aunt Cathy is too much weight for the old mare," she confessed, flatly. "Fine." She locked eyes with Jenifer. "You want to go alone or I can stay and ride with?"

"Go, Momma." Jenifer managed a soft smile. "Get settled in and enjoy the indoor wedding you cooked so much food for."

"That's my girl. No wedding day jitters, now." She turned to Michael, shoving him out the door. "Now you get going!"

"See you on the other side of the bridge, Sissy!" Michael shouted from the stairs, making her giggle.

The mansion seemed quiet in that moment, more than any other time she had been left there alone. Thunder rolled, rain unyielding, and the gusts of wind made the glass panes rattle. A strike lit the room with blinding light, making her flinch. The floorboards underfoot vibrated with the powerful boom and she inhaled swiftly. It was enough to make her hide away from the windows as she ventured out into the hall and down the spiraling staircase. She sat in the receiving room, staring at the old Polish-made grandfather clock that had made it across the Atlantic and survived the Revolutionary War.

At least the old thing still keeps time. Heavens help us if it ever breaks down.

Time ticked by and she stood, pacing. Her brother should have been back by now.

It's been almost an hour.

Pausing, she turned to the front door and threw it open. Despite being midday, an orange hue covered the world out-side. It looked like hell on earth with broken branches scattered about and the white picket fence on the ground in places. The rain stung her face and arms, but she stepped out. Pushing against the gusts of wind, she stumbled into the muddy road, looking toward the farm where she could see the bridge. There were no signs of anyone coming.

Nothing will stop me. Momma spent three days in that kitchen to make this happen. Hell or highwater, my wedding will happen.

She gripped her skirt, hiking it high, and began her march.

The mud proved too much for her shoes, and she abandoned them. A gust of wind slammed her, and she stumbled to the side, barely catching the bridge railing. Glancing up, she could see all the way across the bridge. Her brother was there, calming old Penny who snorted. The buggy sat tilted, a wheel sunken into the mud. Their childhood friends Rory and Claude were trying to pull the buggy out.

Jenifer shouted, but no one seemed to hear her. The river beneath the bridge was choppy and foaming as the salt in the brackish water frothed in the wind. Determined to push on, Jenifer stepped farther onto the bridge. She was already soaked to the bone with her teeth chattering. The farmhouse was just around the bend. Looking at her bare muddy feet, she willed them to move forward. Wind gusts made her skirt flail, and she struggled to stay upright.

Should I turn around...? No. I've made this walk a billion times. I can do this. It's just a thunderstorm...

Each step was arduous as the wind grew stronger. The rain slammed into her, stinging her face like bees, and at last she made eye contact with Michael. Penny reared up, he fell back into the mud, and the others rushed to his side. Jenifer persevered, pushing forward as the old mare ran off around the bend. She was halfway across... The boys could help her from there.

A strange sound met her hears, a cracking and rumbling. This wasn't thunder. This wasn't the wind. The bridge shook, and she looked to the men. They looked down the river, and she saw the whites of their eyes as they began screaming.

RUN! RUN NOW!

She took two strides and slipped, her knee popping. Collapsing to the bridge, she turned. A wall of muddy and debris-laden water came crashing down on her, and the bridge gave way. The water knocked the breath from her. Inhaling brought stinging pain as the saltwater filled her lungs. She tried kicking, but as she twisted and bumped into the unknown, there was no telling up from down. Her knee burned, and the light faded...

More water pressed down on her...

Darkness gripped her.

I can't remember if the snapping sounds came from me or the wooden bridge but... it was so cold. So horribly cold.

7

SHOW MUST GO ON

Morning rehearsal buzzed all around Remi as he scratched his chin. Swallowing, he glared at the rack of tuxedos, mind reeling. When he managed to get an ice pack and brought Bailey to the room, Jenifer had already fallen asleep. She mumbled, tossing and turning from whatever nightmare plagued her. Bailey shooed him out of the master bedroom to his tiny, shared room where he finally fell asleep on the twin bed.

In the morning, he woke to find his roommate Bob pacing the small space. "Wedding day jitters?" chuckled Remi, walking down the hall to the rack of plastic garment bags containing their tuxedos.

Bob paused at his side. "You can say that. Aren't you nervous? I mean, we have no idea who or what we're stuck with…"

"The contract doesn't make us stay with them for life if it doesn't work out." Shrugging, Remi checked the tags on the bags until he found his name. "I hope this fits okay. Unlike my prom tux."

"Man, yeah, you should try this diet I'm on. You gotta cut

all the potatoes out," Bob nodded, locating his own bag. "Trust me, I'm a certified therapist. I know what I'm talking about."

Remi furrowed his brow. "And what do a therapist and nutrition have in common?"

"Oh this sounds like a great joke! I don't know. You tell me." Tucking the bag over his arm, Bob rubbed his hands together, leaning in for the punchline.

Remi's eyes widened. *I feel bad for his bride to be.* "Well look at the time!" His booming voice made Bob leap back a little. "We better get ready for dress rehearsal, Bob!"

"Y-yeah."

Remi scanned the hallway, searching for Jenifer. What they had done—or at least started—last night had been amazing. Unfortunately, she wasn't the bride he had spoken to on the phone. She wouldn't be the one he would be married to. No, instead...

Dammit, I just had to make that deal involving the producer's daughter.

He covered his mouth as he dressed, angry at the blind jump after money. His phone buzzed and the name flashed: *UNKNOWN CALLER.* Sending it to voicemail was followed by two more calls without messages. At last, he silenced his phone. A text popped up from a private number.

[PRIVATE NUMBER: Are you fucking kidding me! You'd rather marry on live television with a stranger than me!]

SHIT. It's that crazy bitch Monica.

He worked fast, not reading anything else as he blocked the number.

I hope the filming location hasn't been leaked. This could be bad.

"Mr. Adama. This way. We will be reviewing some of the scripted parts and what to expect." It was the emo-kid from before.

"Thanks." He shoved the phone in his pocket, following the

intern to the prep area downstairs.

He walked into a room to see that all the chairs were taken. Bob rushed in behind him, and with that, the door shut. Bailey paced in front of the grooms, most sitting, but a few standing at the back like Remi and Bob. Each one locked eyes with her, and she scribbled something on her clipboard. She circled back to the other end of the room, asking a name to confirm she had indeed memorized each groom. As she did so, more writing was recorded, and the men shot looks to one another, their nervousness building. At last, she returned to the front of the room like a coach and inhaled deeply.

"Listen up! We will be taking each of you one at a time to resolve..." they followed her glance to a scruffy, greasy-haired man who shrank in his chair, "...appearance issues. We are going to be on national television, and if we're lucky, picked up globally or at least on Netflix or Hulu. We are taking you first come, first serve. Get comfortable." She turned to her clipboard. "Okay, Stan, you're first. Follow me this way, and we'll get to work. After that, we will allow you a recorded, blind, in-person session with your future wives."

Stan puffed out his chest, a suave clean-cut man in glasses who sashayed out the door, winking at Remi and Bob like he beat them somehow. "Early to rise, they say."

Remi rolled his eyes, muttering under his breath, "Ass kisser."

Bob chuckled. "Right?"

An hour came and went, the chairs opening up. Remi was glad to sit, but annoyed. He had pulled his phone out a few times, but Monica was still attempting to blow it up. The battery was fading fast, and he scoffed. Placing it in his pocket, his mind wandered until at last it settled back on what happened last night. He had nearly killed a woman, possibly twice when her knee buckled in the tub. A smile came to his lips. She had been so fascinating. Never had he met someone so innocent and naughty in one package and he grunted.

Oh, how I wish I could just get one more chance with her before...

"Hey man." Bob slid over to him and tapped his arm, leaning in to whisper, "So you, uh, you watch adult movies?"

Remi's face wrinkled in confusion. "Do you mean porn?"

"Y-yeah... adult movies," he repeated. "Do you, you know, watch them for... uh..."

"Jerking off?" Remi tilted his head, Bob signaling for him to lower his voice. *Wrong conversation to have with someone as loud as me... but where the hell is he going with this?*

"Right, for *release*." Bob's word choice made Remi snort. "I do. Do you?"

Remi squinted his eyes at the man. "Doesn't everyone?"

"Well," Bob glanced around the room, leaning in and lowering his voice further, "I like them, but I don't watch them if they have a man in them."

Remi narrowed his eyes in confusion. "Um, don't most of them have a man in them?"

Bob scowled, face disgusted. "It's not... well, I mean, looking at another man's dick outside of medical reasons seems... it makes me uncomfortable. I'm just afraid..."

Are you out of your mind? Just pretend that's you pounding that big black beautiful babe from behind! With a smirk, Remi nudged him. "I get it, man. You're afraid you might see a huge cock and decide you like looking at one after all."

Dave paled, tripping on his words. "T-that's n-not what I m-meant?!"

"Man, when I watch them, I just think, *yup! That's me! The baseball bat with veins!* And sit back and enjoy the show." Remi's laughter filled the room, making everyone turn.

Bob's face reddened, embarrassment and anger building. "That's not what I meant." He managed to say, voice stern.

Oh, we're angry.

"Look man, I just don't understand the big fear. You ever been in a locker room growing up?" Remi marveled.

"I was home schooled," declared Bob.

That explains everything...

"Bob, you're next." Bailey's voice cut in, and Remi watched her shoo him out the door. A few moments later, she ushered the two final grooms out, but instead of following them, she turned and slammed the door closed, locking it behind her. "Remi."

He stood in alarm. "What's wrong?"

Again, the pacing started as she rubbed her forehead. "She's not here."

"Who?" He was confused.

"Karen." When he gave her a baffled expression, she started again. "Your bride—the producer's step-daughter Karen. She's supposed to be here by now but..."

"Am I not getting married then?" Remi felt a small wave of relief, though he did his best to hide it.

"Well, about that..." Glancing at her clipboard, she flipped a page up and sighed. "We do have a replacement: the girl you met last night." She shot a look his way, and he smirked. She returned the look. "I thought you might like to hear that good news."

"But the contract?" Remi lowered his voice. "I take it this means I'm back to the original rate."

"You still get double." She sat down and crossed her legs. "You get triple if she shows in time."

Remi puffed out his cheeks. *There's the catch. I get the full amount if I marry Karen last minute...*

"But seeing as no one has heard from her, you might have dodged a bullet, Mr. Adama." She folded her hands on top of the clipboard.

"She can't be that bad..." Shoving his hands in his pockets, his hair stood on end as he gripped his cell phone. *Was I about to marry someone like Monica? I would rather forfeit the fucking money.*

"Never mind that." She changed subject. "Jenifer van Winkle seems to be rather excited about it. So sign here." Bailey presented the marriage certificate written out and signed to be with Jenifer van Winkle.

"Really?" He spun away to hide the excitement on his face. *Maybe my luck is changing for once!* "How's her knee doing?"

"On site med said to keep it in the brace and try not to bend it. Gave her some pain killers and trying to keep her off her feet until we need her for filming." Bailey stood, tapping him on the shoulder. He turned back, gripping the pen and signing. "Now, let's get you ready for your bride, Mr. Adama."

"R-right." He thought for a moment and curiosity go the better of him. "How many have pulled out of this in the last twenty-four hours?"

"There's only three couples left." She choked on her words, pausing near the door.

"But we had like twelve grooms?" Remi looked back to the room, counting the men he recalled.

"Their brides backed out during the recorded conversation."

"What in the fuck did they say?"

She puffed out her cheeks, unlocking the door. "I can't disclose that private information to you."

Remi's eyebrows lifted as he watched her leave.

Did they miss out on the fact we are going to be on television, and it was a recorded conversation?

8

LAST CALL

Staring at herself in the mirror, Jenifer didn't know how to feel. They had given her something for the pain in her knee, and it had knocked the ache down, but still she had her leg propped up with ice for swelling. Behind her, the hair dresser was having a hell of a time with the veil they'd chosen for her. She couldn't deny the fact it matched her dress well. Looking to the skirt, she saw that the muddy stains and even the tear had been expertly mended. A tailor had brought the dress back to her, gushing over the vintage quality and refusing to allow anyone to put her in a different dress.

Her heart fluttered. It looked like the day she wore it, and she could almost hear her mother fussing at her all over again. A make-up artist and hair stylist competed for room as they finished preparing her for this *special day*. The excitement of the other brides added to her own, but she paled as thunder rolled and a shutter slapped against the house. Somewhere beyond them, a talking box spoke of the incoming hurricane.

It's happening all over again.

Anxiety crushed her. Her smile faded.

But this time I made it, made it to the farmhouse.

One of the interns came in, drenched even under his poncho. "I lost the damn umbrella. What category are we up to?"

Category? Do they mean the storm has categories? Is it that serious like back when I...

"Just announced it hit category three," sighed another hair dresser, crossing her arms. "They said they were getting gusts up to 112 mile per hour in the Bahamas. Shocked it's not pushing into cat-4."

"Well, ladies," Jenifer jolted as the hair dresser tugging on her hair and veil spoke, "at least this place has a gorgeous dining hall. Those chandeliers are to die for."

"Oh, so true!" agreed a bride, nodding. "I saw it before the setup. Can't wait to see how they dolled it up!"

Jenifer's eyes bounced to each person as she spoke, but her thoughts muted their words. A chill ran through her, the thunder and wind outside rattling the window panes. She inhaled sharply and held it.

I'm alive again, but will the storm sweep me away? Just like last time?

Thunder hit close, the chandeliers rattling, and the other brides yelped. It made her heart race, and she bolted from the chair, ignoring the cries of the stylist. Running past the televisions and dumbstruck staff, she flew up the stairs. She panicked, turning in a circle before running away in long strides, bare feet thudding against the wooden floor.

Bailey flattened herself against the wall to get out of the way of the dashing bride, paling as if a phantom came at her. A shriek filled the hall as Bailey attempted to climb the walls. Remi turned, face curious, just as Jenifer slammed into him.

"Remi!" She realized who the wall of flesh was that had stopped her. "Remi..." Relief filled her, tears welling up as she clenched his tuxedo.

His great big arms wrapped around her. "Let's go someplace private. It seems you scared the shit out of Bailey! She's gasping for air and sunk to her knees in the hall. Come on." He took her hand. "This way."

Jenifer wouldn't let go of his hand, the heat of his body calming her as her shoulders shuddered. He pulled her into a dark room, slamming the door and locking it. At last she pulled away, trying to remove her makeup smudges from his black tuxedo. Gripping her wrists, he tugged her back, then lifted her face with a finger beneath her chin, demanding she look at him. He smiled, and her heart fluttered. A huff escaped him at last as he searched her face.

"Dammit, I wish I had my glasses."

She furrowed her brow. "Where are they?"

He shrugged. "Either on the bridge or in the car. Not sure."

"Oh no, and the storm..." A lightning strike hit close, and she buried herself in him again.

"It seems this has you a little freaked out." He rubbed her back. "Oh, I know what will get your mind off this." His hands gripped her waist and guided her to a desk in the corner.

"I don't think journaling about this will help." Jenifer frowned as the back of her thighs bumped into the dress, the edge softened by the bundled train of the dress.

"That's not what I had in mind," he chuckled, lifting her up to sit her on the desktop.

"I don't understand?" She tilted her head in confusion.

"Oh, you will."

He knelt on the floor before her, making her heart race.

Is... is he proposing?

The heat of his hands slid up her shins, gentle as he caressed her knees, skipping over the brace. She stiffened, gripping the edge of the desk. He pushed her legs apart, squeezing the inside of her thighs with his large hands. Remi paused, thumbing the garter belt.

Wait, that's for...

He moved his hands higher until they found her pussy, rubbing between her folds. She gasped. His finger followed the silken crevasse to the pink pearl. She tried to close her legs in reflex but caught on his broad shoulders. She frowned, hating not being able to see him. Her skirt hid him away, making her rely solely on the sensations and heat of his hands on her body. Slowly, purposefully soft, he circled her clit. Breathing steady, she made herself relax. Closing her eyes, she focused on the pleasure he gave her. The fear that had sent her bolting washed away.

I love how he touches me... Don't stop! Don't ever stop, Remi.

The heat of his breath blew across her pussy, and she throbbed with wanton want. His other hand glided in, rubbing the opening, growing slick with each stroke. At last, he slid a finger inside her wet heat, and she moaned. His stroking added to the pleasure of circling her clit. She spread her legs, wanting to give him more room to play with her. He pressed harder and faster against her swollen jewel. Her legs shook in response, and he began thrusting his fingers quicker, hard and calculated with his circling.

She panted, arching and fighting the urge to close her legs. The rise of an orgasm brought a smile to her face, her eyes closed tight. If the lightning still threatened to strike her down, she had forgotten and paid it no heed. His finger pulled away from her clit, and his tongue took its place. She squealed, biting her lip to hold it in for fear they would be discovered. His fingers abandoned her, leaving her aching until his tongue ran the length of her opening. She moaned. A shiver of pleasure rattled through her entire being. Lips wrapped around her clit, the jolt of her body electrifying. He pulled her to the edge of the desk, leaving her teetering with her legs on his shoulders somewhere beneath the white satin skirt.

Another moan left her trembling lips, his teeth teasing her pearl-sized treasure. Sucking hard and long only made the shaking in her legs increase, the verge of orgasm haunting her. Wanton desire made her pussy ache to have him inside her again. Memories of how good his swollen shaft felt stroking the slick, sensitive...

"Fuck me," she breathed.

He didn't stop his play.

"Please, I want your cock inside me," she begged.

Releasing her jewel, he barked through the skirt. "Not yet. We can't."

"Wait, what?" She released the desk only to grab it again. "R-Remi!"

His fingers slid inside her, and she moaned as he stroked slowly. Dripping wet, she tightened on his fingers, her orgasm nearing its peak. The suckling returned to her clit, shifting so his tongue circled it as his finger had done before. She lurched forward. He switched to two fingers, rubbing in more places, speeding up with each passing second. All at once, she peaked, a wail coming from her as she came hard. She could feel how she squeezed around his fingers and gushed with the wake of her orgasm. He slowed his play, making her ride out the oh-so-sensitive vibrations shooting through her. When Remi climbed out from under her skirt, she had slumped back on the desk, panting. He chuckled as their eyes met.

"We have to save the other for the honeymoon tonight." He shrugged.

"No fair." She swallowed, catching the tightness in his pants. "Are you going to be able to live with that?"

Another shrug. "Something tells me this will be worth the wait when I don't have to keep my tux on."

She laughed. "Thank you for making me... feel better."

The shutter began banging against the side of the building.

Jenifer flew off the desk and back into Remi's arms. He hugged her tight, and for the first time, Jenifer felt alive again. It was as if all that time being dead had been just a distant dream, and she had found her soulmate, the one who could anchor her back into the world.

Did I find my second chance? Is this the man I've been waiting for all this time?

9

GROOM'S BRIDE

Remi was relieved they had escaped into the master bedroom with the fancy bathroom. He washed his face and hands while Jenifer rested on the bed, feeling faint. He lingered until she fell asleep before heading for the door. The storm outside seemed to be taking a physical toll on her. Granted, with a hurricane fueling the weather, they were in for hours of thunder, wind, rain, and potential tornado warnings with flood advisories to boot. Bailey waited outside the room for him, still pale and shaking.

"Are you okay?" Remi rushed to her. "You look like you saw..."

"G-g-g-g-ghost." He almost didn't hear the stuttering whisper.

"Oh! Is this place haunted?" He looked around, excited. "I've never seen a ghost before."

"The bride," she pointed to the door to the room where Jenifer slept. "She's a ghost!"

"That's rather rude." Remi made a face. "I mean, she is rather pale, but..."

Bailey scoffed, pushing past him. "Are you blind?"

"I lost my glasses, so yes, I am blind."

49

Bailey swung the door open, but Jenifer was gone. "Look—vanished."

"Oh, well maybe she's in the bathroom?" Remi started in that direction when water hit him; the window was open. "Oh no, did she... run away?"

"She's. A. Ghost." Bailey held her arms out, eyes wild.

"I don't know what you saw, but maybe you need some sleep." Remi couldn't see any signs of Jenifer outside and closed the window. "What should we do?"

Bailey shivered. "She disappeared, Remi."

"Yeah, out the window. I thought she was asleep in the bed." He reassured himself, scratching his jaw.

"Look, she didn't even leave an impression in the bed, Remi!" Bailey waved her hand out as if to provide evidence.

"Uh, maybe she fixed it before she left," countered Remi. "Look, there's a hurricane unfolding out there. It can't be safe. I'm going after her."

He started for the door, but Bailey grabbed his arm. "She's a fucking ghost. If you leave the premises, your contract is void."

Remi pulled his arm free. "Leaving someone in that storm is a risk I'm not okay with. If you're asking me to choose my money or her life, I choose her life."

Before she could say anything else, he rushed down the hall to the stairs. He pulled the bow tie loose and tossed it to the ground. Flying down the steps, his every footstep thundered through the house. The audio guy carrying the boom mic went to yell at him, and he tossed his jacket in his face. Cameras all turned as he dashed out the doorway, and there was his Focus.

He dipped his hand in his pocket, relief filling him. By some strange fate, he had kept his keys close. Hopping into the car, he spied his glasses and put them on, the world snapping into focus. He didn't care that he was soaked from short jog. All that mattered was that he could *save her*. The little car sputtered to life and he followed the road back toward the bridge where they had met.

The little Focus fought to stay on the road as each gust of wind slammed into it. Cursing under his breath, Remi fought to look all around. The road started to make the turn, and there before the bridge, a woman in white stood. Jenifer turned as if she had been trapped there for some time, trying to decide if she dared cross the bridge. Water splashed up as the little river had doubled in volume. Muddy and white-capped water rose, foaming up and flecking into the wind, and the bridge swayed in the wind.

Her wedding dress whipped around, and Jenifer stumbled as a gust rocked the little car. He flashed the high beams at her, and she frowned. At last, he crept the car closer, and she waited. Sucking on his cheek, he understood at last.

"She's going to make me chase her." He put the Focus in park, inhaling a deep breath. "Okay, my little Runaway Bride. Here I come."

Shoving the door open, he walked slowly, expecting her to take off at any moment. He stopped a few feet away, towering over her in the flashes of lightning. She reached for him, then her fingers retreated. The look on her face, reddened from sobbing, told him something had rattled her. His heart skipped a beat.

"Did I do something wrong?" He feared the answer.

"No, no, you didn't, Remi." She shook her head, not breaking their intense stare.

"Why'd you run?" He looked stern, trying to mask the emotions boiling inside him. *Why'd you run away from me? From us? Didn't you feel we had something special? Something that just felt... like destiny?*

"I didn't." She looked back to the bridge. "But I woke up and found myself back here and..."

"Sleepwalking?" He looked at the bridge, waves managing

to rise and break across the road.

"Not exactly." Again, she reached for him, pausing just shy of gripping his drenched shirt.

He grabbed her hand, her fingers icy in his own. "Then what? Why run away from what we could be? I know it's intimidating getting married on a television show but..."

She laughed. "I love you."

He smiled. "I love you, too."

"No one has ever made me laugh and look forward to the tiniest of moments together as I have with you, but Remi... I'm..."

Lightning hit the Focus, the sound making Remi scoop Jenifer into his arms and start running. She screamed, fingers digging into him as the car burst into flames. A smell of ozone filled the air, making him tighten his hold. They were halfway across the bridge when the road shook beneath them. Jenifer buried her face in his chest, shaking with fear.

"It's happening again," she kept muttering into him.

A tree, swept up by the river, banged against the bridge, unable to flow under or over. Another tree rode on the storm surge wave. Swallowing, Remi held onto Jenifer tight. His car was fucked and popping and now, the bridge was about to be destroyed.

"Hang on! I refuse to die here before we have a chance to even properly get to know one another!" he shouted.

My bad luck seems to be pulling out the stops. Now if my dumb luck can just kick in for this one moment...

The water was starting to flow over the road, making his footing uneasy. He started sliding as they reached the last few strides. The bridge creaked and popped. Another thud, and he was hydroplaning on his feet.

Is this even possible? Fuck me!

He hit the mud along the side of the river, and his balance gave way. Down they both went, sliding across the ground. They scrambled to their feet, faces and clothes covered. The bridge buckled, the storm surge chasing them down the road as it overflowed the river. Remi thanked his luck for the uphill run for the first time in his life. Reaching beside him, he locked hands with Jenifer, and they managed to turn the bend, leaving the water behind. She tugged his hand, and he followed her up a steep driveway. The gates to the mansion had been left open as they slowed down and panted.

Leaning against the brick wall, Remi paused to slow his racing heart. The covered porch gave them very little protection from the rain riding on the nonstop winds of the hurricane. Jenifer searched the bricks. He narrowed his eyes at her, realizing he had cracked one of the lenses in his glasses.

"Shit, that was close!" He had finally caught his breath.

She paused, glancing over at him. "Thank you for that." A brick came loose, and she reached in to produce a key.

Remi stared at her. "Well, that was a lucky guess."

"No, not a guess. Granted, this isn't the type of key I expected. It seems the current owner has been keeping the old tradition alive." She handed the key over.

"Should we knock first?" Remi stared at the key in his palm.

Jenifer pointed at a sign on the window reading:

Will be gone until Thanksgiving. Please do not leave packages at door.—TW

"Huh." Remi tilted his head and pushed the key into the lock. "It's an emergency, and we can't stay out here in a hurricane. We can ask for forgiveness later or just cover our tracks."

"R-Right." Jen gripped the back of his shirt.

The locks turned with ease and opened. With a scrape, the door opened wide, and they walked slowly through the foyer. Water tapped on the floor as it dripped off them and onto the wooden floor, waxed and kept to a historical level. Walking into the receiving room, Remi spun, marveling at the space. The

Victorian furniture, the grandfather clock and its swinging pendulum, even the lamps were kept mimicking a forgotten time.

Jenifer began to cry. She stood before a massive family portrait, covering her mouth. He approached her to see what the matter was when he locked eyes with one of the girls in the painting.

It's her. That's Jenifer in that painting.

His eyes searched the frame and painting until at last he saw what he looked for: *Van Winkle Family, 1840.*

"That's you." He spoke the words at last. "But how is that even possible?"

"Remi." She turned to face him, demanding his eyes. "I've been trying to tell you this since the bridge. I'm a ghost. I've been dead a long time. On a day much like this, storm and all, the bridge broke and swept me away on my way to get married at the farmhouse."

He paled. *What do we do from here?*

10

BRIDE'S GROOM

She waited for the words that would follow, but none came. They stood in silence under her parent's painted gazes. Here she was, home again, but with a different groom than she left to go marry. Her heart raced, and her fingers ached in the cold. She could see Remi's lips turning blue, and he shivered. Panic drove her as she grabbed his arm and tugged him along.

"You're freezing."

Opening a door down the hall behind the stairs, she flustered. The bathroom had been demoed out and, from the look of it, sat that way for some time. A note on the wall said: *Use upstairs bathroom.* She spun Remi around and shoved him up the stairs in a rush. Relief washed over her to see the bathroom there had been remodeled completely.

"Come on. Let's get you warmed up."

She had managed to figure this out at the farmhouse, so she turned the knobs properly. The large walk-in shower wasn't as massive, but the Jacuzzi-style bathtub had been rather tempting. Shaking that from her thoughts, she doubled down on caring for the still silent Remi. The stream of water grew warmer under her fingers as Remi stared at himself in the mirror.

"Am I dead too?"

"No, you're very much alive... for now." Pulling him into the shower, she pulled his glasses off and placed them gently on the vanity. "Come on, big guy. You need to warm up."

Back in the shower under the warm water, she began washing the mud from his face and hair. He smiled at her, wiping her mud-covered cheek. Before she could say to stop, his lips locked with hers. He deepened the kiss and began undoing the back laces of her wedding dress. Her wanton desire surfaced in an instant, her fingers desperate to unbutton his shirt. At last, the muddy clothes thumped onto the shower floor.

His hands gripped her ass, bringing her wet, naked body against his. She could feel his cock growing hard between them, and for once, she was the warm one. She licked into his mouth, wanting to play with his tongue, explore his body, hear him moan like he had before...

Thunder roared somewhere outside, and they paused, looking at one another.

"For a ghost, you're pretty hot." Remi's blue lips were gone, the shivering ceased.

"For a groom, you're pretty brave," she retorted.

He laughed and began kissing her neck. "You think the owner will mind if we spend our honeymoon night here?"

"As a previous tenant, I'm sure I can convince him that it's purely for personal preference," she cooed, enjoying the way his hands explored her body. "So, are you really trying to make love to a dead girl?"

"Everything I know about the living says you're not-so-dead." Chills rattled her as his kisses trailed across her collarbone.

Hot hands squeezed her breasts, then he licked and suckled her nipples, tasting one then the next. Satisfied with his sampling, his hands flowed down her torso, finally dipping between her thighs. She leaned into him, still sensitive from the session on the desk. A finger rolled over her clit, and all the pleasure flooded through her. Her shoulders shook, and she slid her hand down his body. She gripped his hard cock, her pussy throbbing with need.

Fuck this foreplay...

"W-wait," she said out loud. Swallowing her fear, she prepared herself for what she wanted to voice. "Not yet. I want you on the bed."

Again, he tilted his head as a sparkle came to his eyes. "Me on the bed?"

"Yes. I want to..." She cleared her throat, reaching behind him to cut off the water, "...be in charge."

He nodded his head, mulling it over a moment. "I can get on board with that idea."

A grin stretched across her face as she pulled him along. Toweling off, they ventured through the upstairs hallway naked. Jenifer stopped before a door, and her giggles stopped. Her chest ached as she ran her hand over it. At last, she turned the old knob and pushed the door open. The bedroom inside looked...

"Wait, why...?" She lost her words, pushing inside the room and looking all around.

"Was this your room?" Remi strutted in behind her.

"More like..." Taking in the room, she found no detail missed or preserved. "It *is* my room. Someone kept it the same for... I don't even know how many years."

"Well, if the picture downstairs is accurate... it's pushing almost two hundred years," offered Remi.

Jenifer covered her mouth. "I'm a cradle robber."

Remi lost it, breaking into an explosion of laughter.

A letter drew her attention, the paper resting on the bed, her name clear across the top:

To Jenifer van Winkle,

May you find a way to sleep upon your bed again with the right groom of your choosing.

Your great, great nephew,

Timothy van Winkle

"Wait, who got you into this?" Jenifer spun, showing Remi the letter.

"Timmy... do you think he knew something?" Remi marveled, a half-grin on his face.

"He must've known something because..." She looked down at her pale, curvy body. "I am very much back alive again."

Remi dropped the letter and kissed her again. He pushed her back until he backed her into the bed. Again, his groped her breasts, but she pulled him away. Baffled, he furrowed his brow. Gripping his shoulders, she switched where they stood. When she managed to circle him with the bed behind him, she shoved him down. He sat, a look of excitement growing on his face. Pushing him onto his back, she crawled on top of him, kissing him. Sucking on his tongue, she wanted to be in charge of this next session. Her knee had stopped hurting, bending easily once more, and she wouldn't let this opportunity be missed. She caught his tongue in her teeth when he ventured. Releasing him, she let him retreat a little.

"Good." She gripped his cock and stroked the length of his shaft. "Because I now own this."

Remi's eyes widened, and he fell silent.

Crap, did I overstep? I just... I just want to show him how much I enjoy him and want to please him. What if I'm being too much?

"Am I being too aggressive?" she asked.

"You did sign the paperwork to own it." He gripped her breasts. "Does that mean I own these now?"

She laughed. "Maybe?"

His voice deepened, his hands pulled her into him, and his

lips tickled at her ear. "Look—be aggressive. I don't mind. Be creative."

The tension in her shoulders relaxed. "Then I'll take my time."

Remi's body tensed a little under her, his cock pushing into her palm where she still gripped him. Releasing him, she grabbed his wrists and pinned them above his head. Her fingers trailed down his arms, and he shuddered under her. Leaning in, she kissed him once more before nibbling on an ear. Another shudder and he tensed, his cock growing harder between their bodies. She began sucking on his nick, and he shifted. She could see he enjoyed every touch she gave him.

"Oh, this is a new venture for me," he gruffed, leaning his head to give her more room.

She sucked long and hard, leaving a hickey by the time she released. Venturing slow and agonizing downward, she relished leaving the marked trail. Tiny bursts of purple and red fireworks blossomed across his neck, down his chest, and snaked down his torso. She licked and sucked, kissing and worshipping his body as if daring to gobble him up. He moaned, covering his eyes with a forearm.

With a grin, she ran her tongue from base to tip across the underbelly of his dick. He grunted, the precum dripping down the side. Her tongue circled the mushroomed tip, and his body tensed. She had slid back off the bed some, running her hands along the inside of his thighs and squeezing. Again, she taunted him with long, sultry licks on all sides of his cock until at last, she began kissing his taut skin. She teased him with her lips, licks of her tongue, and the subtle sucking as if she aimed to French kiss his dick. A moan escaped him, his toes curling.

Squeezing his thigh, she rested her lips around the tip of his cock, tongue circling. She mimicked the speed that he had used for her clit. Remi took a deep breath and held it. Another squeeze of his thigh, and an audible sound of pleasure escaped his lips as the breath broke free. She wanted to hear him, wanted to make him beg for her to stop, only for her to continue until he exploded over and over again. His dick jumped, every finished rotation enhancing the tension in his body.

Like they say about marriage: What's his is hers, and what's hers is hers.

11

DEFINITION OF LUCK

The heat of Jenifer's lips against the tip of his dick made him ache. His balls drew in, the agonizing desire to thrust further into the depths of her mouth was driving him crazy. Granted, the sexual torture and build had been amazing. Never had a woman blessed his body like she had. The way she made love to all of him was exhilarating. Her tongue circled the end of his dick, and he tightened his fist. He had to fight the urge to take over. Never had he wanted to release so badly in his life, yet he still wanted more of her play.

I want to come so badly, but I don't want this to end.

At last, her lips slid down to the base of his shaft. His body shuddered, on fire with the electrifying pleasure it brought him. She sucked long and hard, tongue wiggling under his shaft in the wet heat of her mouth. As slowly as she had taken all of him in, she rose up and off with a pop of her lips. A grunt escaped him, his balls tightening. The heat of her finger started to massage them as her lips slid back down his hardened length. This time she pushed him to the back of her throat, rocking her head back before sliding up and off again.

This feels amazing but agonizing all at once.

"You can't come yet," she ordered. The heat of her breath on his wet cock made it jerk.

Her tongue licked the side, her play with his balls still unfolding. Another squeeze of his thigh made him grunt. In his mind, he wondered if he might just release without even being inside her at all. The French kissing of his cock started once more, and his toes curled. His body stiffened, the urge to release so hauntingly close that he whimpered.

Jenifer broke away, leaving a rush of cool air to slam into him. Before he could take his arm off his eyes to see where or what she intended to do next, she was back to kissing his neck. Her pussy, wet and hot, began grinding against his cock's length. Another groan escaped him as she repeated a snaking trail of hickeys down his chest. Remi didn't care. He wanted to know how rough and demanding she would be, how long she would dare to keep him lingering in this state of want and need for release.

Halfway down his torso, she sat up, straddling him and pinning his dick between them under her. Removing his forearm, Remi met her provocative glare. His eyes fell to her hands where she groped her breasts, the sight only increasing his arousal. He slid his hands over her thighs, but she reached down and stopped them. Taking his wrists, she pinned them against the bed at his side. A wild grin and mischief filled her face. Leaning down, she kissed him deeply. Her hips shifted, the tip of his cock lining up with her wet pussy.

Tilting his hips, he managed to slide just the tip in, and even at this shallow depth, she could tighten on him. He shifted further, but she matched it and kept him from sliding deeper inside. Grunting with frustration, his smile broke their kiss.

"Not yet. We will get to that later." The voracious tone in her voice made his heart race. "I want..." Her eyes fell to his lips. "I want to sit on your face."

Remi cleared his throat, enamored with the confession. "Oh boy."

Jenifer flinched. "Too much?"

"No." He shook his head. "A little uncouth and raunchy, but I'm into it."

She kissed him once more, sucking on his tongue before pulling away and letting go with a pop. "I'll make this next part well worth it for you."

His heart fluttered. *I might die a happy man with a hardon and blue balls and I don't fucking care. Let's do this!*

She spun around, quick and calculating as her knees rested against his shoulders. Her fingers gripped his cock as she lowered her wet and swollen pussy to his lips. Remi decided to be just as aggressive as she had been with him. Fingers tightened on his dick, a yelp of pleasure escaping her as he licked between the folds to her bean and back again, eating her like a starved animal. She rewarded him by pulling his cock back into the warmth of her mouth, suckling and thrusting him in and out. They moaned into each other. Her drool dribbling hot across his balls had him fighting the urge to come.

She rocked forward, deep throating his cock as she squeezed his balls. He sucked on her clit, and she moaned on his dick. He teased her swollen clit gently with his teeth while muffling her scream on his cock. Tilting his hips, he began thrusting in and out of her vocal attempts of peaking pleasure. Again, he wrapped lips around the pink pearl and sucked, hard and long. Another grunt, and she deep throated him. At last, his pleasure spilled forth.

He moaned into her pussy as he came. Her tongue wiggled, and she swallowed with each release, but she didn't stop. Lips suckling and sliding up and down his overly sensitive shaft sent him into a louder response. She began grinding on his face, and he licked her up, still moaning as she made his orgasm linger in agonizing height. At any moment, his hard-on would be lost, but something about the way she licked his dick just made him stay so hard.

I've never lasted this hard after...

Thoughts fell apart as he came again.

Shit!

A fire of arousal made him both numb and sensitive all at once. It suddenly hit him, what she had said before...

"What if I told you I might know a way to speed things along?"

He licked her deeply, and she hummed on his cock. Faster and faster, her lips slid over the swollen shaft. Again, he came back to her clit, and she went deep down on his dick.

If she can keep me...

They both shuddered with the pleasure they bestowed upon one another. He wanted to release again, so soon, but he fought it back. At last, she broke away. Both panted as she turned, straddling his waist again. She lowered her pussy onto his dick. Her hands caressed his chest and torso, and he gripped her hips, shifting his hips to slide a little deeper. Leaning back on his thighs, she took one hand and began playing with herself.

OH she feels amazing...

The rocking on his hips added to how his cock rubbed inside her tight pussy.

"W-wait!" Remi paled. "Shouldn't we get a condom? Can a ghost get... pregnant?"

Jenifer paused. "Wanna find out?"

"Wow." Remi rubbed his eyes. "You're fearless."

Jenifer shrugged. "It seems I have a second chance at love, and life, and well...we are married."

Remi nodded, pondering her situation and his own. "You know we may not get the money."

"I've got a mansion?" she offered.

Remi looked around. "I suppose I can set up my home business here."

She laughed, leaning down to whisper in his ear. "And I look forward to haunting your cock."

He laughed. "And something tells me you mean that." Wrapping his arms around her, they kissed. "Seriously though, are we really going to see what happens?"

"Why the fuck not?" She kissed him again, deeper this time. *I've always wanted a kid... and who better to take this path with...?* "But we just met. I almost ran you over."

"You couldn't run me over," she corrected.

"But now you're saying you want to have a kid with me, a complete stranger?" He could see the frustration building on her face.

"You're right... we barely know..." She tried to pull away but found he hugged her tighter. "Look, let me go..."

He nuzzled her ear, his voice deep. "Beg me for my cock, like you did that first night."

She froze.

"Tell me how badly you want it," he continued as his cock throbbed inside her. "I never want this to end."

"Please..." Her hips grinded against him. "Please give it to me."

He kissed her neck. "Give what to you?"

"Please, Remi..." She tried to sit up, but he kept her body pressed against his. "Please cum inside me."

A smile curved his lips, his heart racing. *I don't think I've ever heard a woman beg for that, and I kind of like it.*

"Fuck me until you cum inside!" Her voice sent excited shivers through him. "I want to make babies with you."

He froze. "Wait, what?" *Did she just say...?*

"I want to make babies with you?" She tensed. "Was that too much?"

Laughter rolled out of him like thunder. "You kill me."

"I'm sorry. That was too awkward." Jenifer buried her face into his shoulder.

"No kidding," he chuckled. "Shall we try again?"

Lifting her face, she kissed him, her hands pressed against his cheeks. "I love you. If this is how you solve problems, I will follow you to the ends of the earth, Remi."

Sighing, he searched her eyes. "You know..." She was so close he could actually see her face clearly. "...I like that idea."

Yeah, we may have just met, but something in my gut says she's the one I've been hoping for. Maybe my luck finally caught up to me...

12

RAW CONFESSIONS

I *love this man.*

Jenifer kissed Remi, dipping her tongue between his lips. She rocked against him, regaining their lost sexual momentum. He still wouldn't allow her to sit up. She tried once more, but his large arms hugged her tighter, her breasts aching from their closeness. His knees lifted, and before she fathomed what he planned on doing, he began fucking her hard. Her body arched, allowing his cock deeper inside her. An orgasm exploded from her, and she tightened around his rock-hard cock.

With each thrust, she could feel the gush of her pussy. Remi began to moan, his dick swelling for a moment, adding to her rising orgasm. Her voice cried out, visceral in the moment as he pushed hard inside her. His cock jerked, the rush of hot cum filling her as she gasped. He slowed his rocking hips, teasing her like she had done with him before. They were both breathless with her still laying on top of him, neither willing to move.

He rubbed her back, and at last, inhaled a deep breath and released it, slowing his breathing. Jenifer cuddled against him, listening to his thudding heart. It sounded like the hooves of a horse trotting across a bridge. After a while, she sat up to find Remi fast asleep. Smiling, she eased away and folded her blanket over him. It didn't completely cover his haphazardly placed body, but it would keep him warm for the time being.

She tip-toed to the wardrobe, opening it to find an array of modern clothes. Again, a note pinned to a skirt made her smile:

Aunt Jeni,

Hope at least some of these tickles your fancy. There will be food downstairs, and a credit card in the far left drawer under the microwave.

Timmy

Looking back to the variety of clothing, she muttered, "What in the hell is a credit card and microwave?"

Remi rolled in his sleep, making the bed squeak. He had managed to burrito himself in the blanket now. Peering back into the wooden wardrobe, she grabbed a skirt and a rather skimpy tank top. She liked this new fashion, had seen it a few times on women driving by or even jogging down the road. Slipping them on, she was out the bedroom door and racing down the stairs.

My, these are so much more.. freeing! And they weigh nothing! No more hoops or corsets, no more lacing. It just pulls on and stretches as needed! How amazing clothes have become!

Tears filled her eyes as she stumbled to a stop in the kitchen. It was so different and grand. The white countertops sparkled, and the sink had a long gooseneck spout. She rushed to the deep sink and marveled over how many pans it could fit all at once.

I could hide dirty dishes in this—it's so deep!

Turning around, she saw many objects she hadn't encountered before. Large metal boxes of varying size caught her curiosity. This largest when opened was cold inside, much like the ice boxes her cousins kept certain times of the year. Food and milk were in strange boxes and containers with colors and writing. She shut that door. The next two seemed to do nothing but light up when the doors were opened.

How strange! Wait, is that... is that a chocolate cake? Oh, maybe later... First, I want to see what the other metal boxes have inside.

Shutting the door, she realized the box said *oven* but had no place for wood or coal.

These all just have racks, but I have no idea what for. I have so much to learn about a kitchen... I wonder if Remi can cook?

The other box said microwave, and she opened the drawer beneath it. Inside were menus and a tiny hard red rectangle with *Timothy van Winkle* embossed into it.

How does this work? Why would anyone want this?

"So this is a credit card..." She flipped it over and over, but it was beyond her. "I'll have to ask Remi how to use this later."

"JENIFER?" Remi voice made her drop the card and slam the drawer closed. "JENIFER!"

He's awake! That was a quick nap!

"IN HERE!" She walked to the entryway. "Remi?"

"WHERE ARE YOU!" His voice echoed through the house.

"Wow, you're loud." She blinked as he wandered butt-naked to the top of the stairwell.

"Yeah, my voice carries for miles." He shrugged, coming downstairs. "Or so I've been told by the neighbors."

"Oh! Oh no." She covered her mouth.

"What's wrong?" He rushed to her, grabbing her shoulders.

"You don't have any clothes." She tried not to laugh at the realization.

"Oh shit." He smirked. "But were you going to even give me the chance to put any on?"

She rolled her eyes and paused when her eyes caught on the old Victorian chair. "You know, that's a good point."

I've always wanted... could we? Why not? After all, this is technically our wedding day... Glancing at the clock, she corrected, *my wedding night.*

He followed her gaze. "Wow, it's already night, huh?" Sashaying past her, he called back. "You hungry? Whoa, check out this kitchen!"

Without any hesitation, Remi started opening and closing cabinets and more. He pulled various items out, laying them on the island counter. Jenifer watched with fascination as he conjured his magic before her. His twisting of knobs and retrieval items from all over left her in awe. He produced eggs without chasing chickens, a flame with no match, and even ingredients she hadn't seen him conjure. He chopped cheese, vegetables, and meat with speed and accuracy. Propping her chin up with her elbows, she watched the wonderous naked chef perform before her.

"Sorry I can't do bacon... or take advantage of those pork chops in there," he announced, mixing eggs. "I'm a little too exposed to risk grease popping and ruining both our night-time fun."

"What are you making, then?" she asked, watching as he added butter to the hot pan, rolling it around.

"Eh, a sort of Western omelet. They didn't have tomatoes or onions." Shrugging, he focused on the task at hand.

Jenifer's stomach grumbled, and her heart skipped a beat. *When was the last time I felt hungry?*

A plate with a perfectly made omelet slid into place, and she took in the glorious smell. The first bite of buttery, fluffy egg with a hint of green pepper and cheese fueled her desire to eat. By the time he finished making his own, joining her on the stool next to her, she had finished a good two-thirds. By the time she cleaned her plate, she realized he had watched her. Slowly, taking another bite of his own omelet, he smiled at her with a sparkle in his eyes.

"You're so damn cute." He snort-giggled and turned to his own meal. "I'll keep cooking for you as long as you keep enjoying my food like that. Deal?"

"Deal." She smiled, stretching with satisfaction. "Thank you. I feel much better."

He was nearing the end of his omelet. "So, I saw you staring at the clock. Was that some epic heirloom?"

Jenifer's face flushed. "I was staring at the chair."

"The chair?" He took one more bite before sliding the plate away.

"Well, besides being the last place I ever sat…" Her fingers balled some of her white cotton skirt to soothe her nervousness.

Remi narrowed his eyes at her. "Were you waiting on someone that day?"

Her eyes shot up to his, paling. "I was waiting on my brother to come get me for my wedding."

Eyes wide, Remi straightened. "Damn. Didn't make it pass the bridge, right?"

Jenifer nodded, her eyes falling across his naked body. "How can you sit there so casually naked like this?"

He shrugged. "What choice do I have? My clothes are in the shower upstairs and I wasn't going to try to walk down those stairs wrapped in that big ass quilt."

Shaking her head, she laughed. "Right."

"So the chair?" He circled back. "Was that all just the memory? I half-expected you to mention your mom or dad."

"N-no, but…" Once more, her face flushed. "I was thinking *we* could use the chair for *something*."

He smirked, lifting an eyebrow. "Oh?"

"Never mind. I'm just being awkward." She turned away. *What the hell am I thinking? Why would he think this idea is sexy at all?*

The heat of his palm slipped up her leg and thigh. She

71

turned on the stool, gasping as his fingers began rubbing between the folds of her pussy. He pressed his lips hard against hers. She deepened the kiss, and his fingers slid inside her. A moan escaped her lips, and she could feel his hard cock rub against her knee. The very idea had invoked a physical reaction.

He wants me like I want him. That desire to explore one another, to bring pleasure upon him in any way I can manage. I've never felt loved or love so strong for someone until I met him. Every moment self-sacrificing and unquestioning. How precious of a person you are, Remi.

13

HAUNTED HOUSE

He loved how her tongue forced its way into his mouth only to coax his own to be caught between her suckling lips. Abandoning his initial play, he knew she was wet and ready. He thought of her growing excitement at the thought of him and her... *on that chair? I think I can accommodate that little fantasy.*

Scooping her up in his arms, Remi stood up from the stool. Jenifer hung onto his neck, eagerness on her face. He stopped in front of the chair.

Crap. Do I put her in the chair or do I sit or...?

"You think I could still sit on it if you're sitting there?" It seemed she was trying to figure the logistics out as well.

"You mean my cock?" He let her down on her feet. "I don't know if I'm hard enough for that."

"I can fix that."

She pushed on his chest, and he fell into the chair. It was wide enough for her to could spread his legs open, kneeling before him. The way her skirt flared out all around her only added to his rising desire. Her warm palm and finger wrapped around his dick, rubbing and stroking. They locked eyes, and she smiled. Leaning in to where her breath washed over his cock sent a shudder through his shoulders. Her nipples were hard under the thin tank top. Licking his lips, he wanted to suckle them, to tease them between his teeth once more.

She blew a stream of air across the underbelly of his cock, still stroking him with her fingers. His eyes were back on her own, and she opened her plump lips. Goosebumps rolled over him as he watched her lick him from base to tip. It had felt so amazing earlier, but watching it now added a new layer of arousal. A second lick took his breath away, and his body tensed with provocative want. His fingers gripped the chair arms. Another lick, and he shifted to press his cock firmly against her tongue.

Fucking glasses... I need to invest in some damn contacts because I would pay good money for a less foggy version of what I am watching her do to my dick. Son of a bitch.

Her tongue circled the mushroom cap, and he groaned. With agonizing slowness, she slid her lips over and down the length of his cock. Before the tip hit the back of her throat, he gave a disapproving grunt. She made a pop as she let go and grinned. Wet with her saliva, her stroking fingers brought on greater pleasure. She twisted her hand, the tips of her fingers sliding across new places.

Fighting the urge to close his eyes, he watched her again take his cock into her mouth. She didn't rush any part of the blow job, and he wouldn't dare disrupt it. Every moment added to his pleasure, his blood rushing as he fought the urge to push deeper down her throat. He wanted to linger on this agonizing edge, savoring each passing moment, drowning in the way she toyed with him.

I could die a happy man...

Pulling away, she stood, clearly debating which way to face. He laughed, pulling her onto him so she faced his chest. Placing her hands on his shoulders, he was quick to have his hands under her skirt and pull her into position. She slid her knees forward, skin pressed against his thighs and into the back of the chair, and he ran his hands along her curves, piling the skirt at her waist. Her pussy was dripping wet as he guided himself inside.

"But the skirt..." She shifted in the chair for a better angle.

"Fuck me in your skirt," he told her.

She blinked, but he throbbed inside her, and she tightened in response. "As you wish, husband."

"I fucking love you."

She laughed, gripping his shoulders tight as she began to rock her hips slowly back and forth. "You feel so damn good."

Weaseling his hands out of the skirt, he watched the plea-sure on her face with each tilt of her hips. He goaded her to change method, and at last, she bounced up and down. His cock hard inside her, she moved him in and out of her. She began moaning, arching her back as she closed her eyes, head tilted back. Pulling at her tank top, he freed a breast and latched onto her nipple. Hungry, he supported her angle, allowing her to rely on the strength of his arm to bring them both deeper pleasure.

He moaned into her breast, and her fingers gripped the back of his head, keeping him there suckling and teasing. She found a combination of rocking and bouncing, his cock growing harder with each thrust. Her skirt fluttered with each drop and rise, and all at once, they peaked together. Both moaned as her thighs hugged his hips. He pushed hard into her, panting, rocking into the last of the orgasm.

They relaxed, and she leaned back with a wondrous smile.

"Is that what you wanted?" he asked, hands running down her back.

"Yeah..." She bit her lip in thought before voicing the curi-osity haunting her. "Where else can we have sex, you think?"

Remi's eyebrows raised high. "You want to go around having sex on furniture?"

She shrugged, batting her eyes at him. "Yeah, I kind of do."

With that, he lifted her off his lap and rose from the Victorian chair. Peering up the stairs then back to the kitchen, his mind raced. Looking back to Jenifer, he frowned. She was rubbing her knee, the swelling kneecap making it clear that he would have to be more mindful with the next spot for intercourse to unfold.

The bed is out of the question. Oh the counter top but... she may not want to bend that knee. Oh, I know!

Without warning, he chucked her over his shoulder. Up the stairs he went with her giggling the whole way. They reached the bedroom, and he put her back on her feet in front of the mirror-topped dresser. She glanced around with a confused expression. When he gestured for her to turn around, she saw him standing naked behind her.

"Your knee doesn't like to bend, right?" He smiled at her in the mirror.

"Right." Her breath caught as his hands snaked in front of her.

One traveled up and beneath her top to grope a breast. The other dove under the waistband of her skirt, sliding between her thighs to her already sensitive clit. She stiffened, and he moved them closer to the dresser. His breath poured over her shoulder, and goosebumps rippled across her skin. Her palms landed flat on the dresser as he played with her, massaging her breast. He loved being able to watch her face as he touched her.

"Is this an okay angle?" His hands retreated to her hips. "Your knee okay if...?"

"Fuck me."

"My pleasure." He smirked.

Pulling up the back of her skirt, he bunched it on top of her hips. The tip of his cock rubbed against the opening of her pussy. She bent over deeper, an arm on top of the dresser. It was more than enough for him to slip inside her pink folds. They moaned together as he slid inside her. His grip on her hips tightened, and he caught her gaze in the mirror.

He gave her a stern look. "Fast and hard this time, then you rest your knee. Got it?"

"Yes, sir."

He pulled back, watching his cock slide back like the hammer on a revolver. When they locked gazes in the mirror again, it was the last thing he saw. The heat spilled over him, the pleasure of his cock thrusting in and out, hard and fast. Her eyes clenched, Jenifer gripped the dresser, thighs bouncing against the lip of the dresser. The mirror wobbled, threatening to break free. Remi shoved forward, releasing with a groan. Her pussy tightened on him, a gush of wet heat soaking his thighs as the mirror cracked.

"Oh no!" Jenifer pulled up and away as the shards fell across the dresser. "That's bad luck!"

"If that means seven years of bad luck for me having you haunting my dick, is it really bad luck at all?" Remi marveled.

They laughed, the adrenaline keeping them going as he pulled her to the bed. Laying side-by-side, he pulled her into him. She smelled wonderful, like peach blossoms in spring. Fighting the weight of sleep, he let his daydreams fill his mind before he dared to voice them at last.

"I think I like the idea of making a mini-me or mini-Jen." He sighed.

"You promise to cook, right? I'll make the babies; you make the dinner." She held his arms around her.

"I'll cook everything but fish," he offered. "I'm allergic."

"Gross. I hate fish."

"My God, where have you been all my life?" he breathed.

"Stuck on a bridge waiting for you to come pick me up, apparently."

EPILOGUE

Two women raced up the muddy slope and fought one another to enter the old farmhouse. The television crew turned, catching the cat fight rolling into the receiving room where Bailey guffawed over the shrieking, wet duo. At last, the weight of the eyes in the room was enough to make them let go of one another's hair and make an attempt to straighten their drenched clothes.

Both had blonde pixie cuts, and the overdone makeup had a few of the crew whisper-wondering if they were siblings. They both peered around, but one stepped forward. Pointing a zebra-striped manicured finger, she came full force at Bailey.

"You! You're the agent in charge of my contract." She snatched the name tag on Bailey's lanyard, jerking the woman forward. "My stepfather put me up to this, and I expect to be treated as a guest of honor."

"K-Karen?" Blinking, Bailey jerked her tag back. "Where have you been? You were supposed to be here days ago."

"Well, my flight to Hawaii got cancelled, and I figured why not go through with this? At least I might become famous." She

78

looked around and pointed at the emo-intern. "Are you Remi?"

"No," Bobby scoffed.

"Hey, bitch, Remi belongs to me." The other woman at last spoke up, the camera man still recording since the fight during their grand entrance.

"What?" Karen spun to shriek at Bailey. "You let him marry her? She was riding my ass all the way from Gainesville!"

"N-no." Bailey marveled over the squabbling women. "I don't even know who *she* is?"

"Bitch, I'm Monica."

Silence fell over the room. Thunder rumbled, and Monica heaved her double-D breasts, stretching the tiger-striped tank top to its limits. Eyebrows lifted around the room, everyone watching to see if the fabric might give way. A feral cat-like hiss erupted from her hot pink lips as she shoved past Karen. The producer's step-daughter lost her balance and landed in the arms of two stagehands who pushed the woman back to her feet for fear she might bite.

"Where is my Remi?" Monica backed Bailey against the wall. "I am here to take what is mine home! How dare he marry someone other than me!"

Bailey paled, then cleared her throat. "He's not here."

"Wait!" Karen joined Monica. "Isn't that the lame-ass home business douche I was supposed to marry for extra cash?"

"He married for money?" Everyone could see the whites of Monica's eyes. "But I have money!"

Clearing his throat, Bobby stepped into the open. "Like she said, he's long gone. We think he got washed away on the bridge."

"WHAT?" Monica spun on her stiletto heels with the grace of a pole dancer.

"His car was on fire. They said lightning hit it."

"Wow... talk about bad luck." Karen shuddered. "Poor bastard."

"They didn't find his body but..." Everyone paled, the silence this time eerie and unsettling as eyes darted away. Hail Marys started around the room as several crew members crossed themselves.

"What's the matter with all of you?" Karen walked up beside Monica, former anger subdued into curiosity.

"What the fuck happened to my Remi?" Monica's Boston accent had boiled to the surface.

Bobby waved for them to follow him upstairs. No one dared to follow the trio. He led them down the hall and into the master bedroom. On a desk was a small LED screen and desktop computer. He sat down, booting it up as the two glared at one another, claws out again. The window suddenly blew open, the rain and wind kicking up with the residual bands of the hurricane that had raged for days.

"Look, I would have been here sooner, but the bridge was out," Karen started, feeling the need to justify herself.

"We seriously think he and the ghost bride were washed away." The intern's words dropped like a stone.

"Ghost bride?" Monica scoffed, rolling her eyes. "You can't be serious."

"Look, this is the last footage we have of him." Bobby twisted back to the two women, their arms crossed and faces unamused. "They didn't know we had hidden cameras in some of the rooms. I swear to you, two people walked into this room that night. I saw her, touched her, hell—even wanted to have sex with that woman in white. None of us knew she was a ghost yet." He frowned, crossing his arms. "Bailey certainly has a signature clear as day on that marriage certificate she mailed out."

"Oh my... this is stupid." Karen started to walk out of the room. "First that whole Blue Lady ghost story, and now this. I am going home. Fuck this."

Bobby turned back to the computer, pulling up the video,

and Karen paused, curious now. Both women leaned in. The frozen frame showed Remi in drenched clothes carrying an armful of toiletries and sweats. He seemed to be talking to someone or something as he marched in. There, floating in the middle of the screen, was a light orb. Monica practically climbed over the emo-intern to rewind the video, cranking up the volume as they watched the conversation play out with a single entity in the room. He had pushed the orb into the room.

"Alright!" Remi said loudly.

He closed the door and rushed to unload his arms onto the bed. The orb hovered close behind him for a moment before travelling to the door and back to him. Remi glanced over his shoulder and smiled, turning back to divide the items evenly as if for two people.

"There, I suppose you should use the shower first," he announced to the orb. "W-wait, what are—"

Static popped and clicked, a faint voice disrupted by the ruined audio.

"Look, we just met and..." Remi stumbled, looking at something as the orb brightened. At last, he whispered, "Dammit, you're gorgeous."

They could see Remi's breath in the air as a shudder shook his shoulders. His pants fell to the floor. He jolted in surprise, stopping by the bed. He sat in alarm, shaking his head as if agreeing to something. Pulling off his shirt, he muttered about his missing glasses. The video scrambled and ended with pops and a click.

"Wait, what happened?" Monica shook the mouse,

rewinding the video to watch it again. "Where's the rest?"

"That's all we got. After that, not another hidden camera worked. We didn't check the footage until way after." He turned to look at Karen, who was on her way out the door.

"First, Mark Wilder, now this Remi guy..." Karen bitched. "Fuck this! I'm going home."

The End

Honey Cummings

A passionate, award-winning author of Fantasy, Honey has turned her aim towards erotica. Blending everyday scenarios and crafting them into steamy, blood-boiling moments for every shade of audience. Whether you want something short and hot like a student-teacher hook up to the more paranormal flair where Sleep with Sasquatch has unexpected bonus, look forward to erotic short stories, novellas, and hopefully a Trilogy in the future. Honey's debut erotic short landed No. 3 in Urban Erotica and continues to satisfy readers time and time again. Be sure to leave her a review and let her know what you think!

https://www.amazon.com/Honey-Cummings/e/
B07WFX5FDX
www.AuthorHoneyCummings.com
instagram.com/authorhoneycummings
twitter.com/HoneyCummings2
facebook.com/
Author-Honey-Cummings-101408818012749

More Honey Cummings Books

Sleeping with Sasquatch
Cuddling with Chupacabra
Naked with New Jersey Devil
Laying with the Lady in Blue
Wanton Woman in White
Beating it with Bloody Mary

Beau and Professor Bestialora
The Goat's Gruff
Goldie and Her Three Beards
Pied Piper's Pipe
Princess Pea's Bed
Jack's Beanstalk
Pulling Rapuzel's Hair

4 Horsemen Publications Erotica

Dalia Lance
My Home on Whore Island
Slumming It on Slut Street
Training of the Tramp

72% Match
It Was Meant To Be... or Whatever

Chastity Veldt
Molly in Milwaukee
Irene in Indianaolis

4HorsemenPublications.com